CAIRO KELLY

AND THE MANN

KRISTIN BUTCHER

ORCA BOOK PUBLISHERS

National Library of Canada Cataloguing in Publication Data
Butcher, Kristin.

    Cairo Kelly and the Mann

ISBN 1-55143-211-0

I. Title.

PS8553.U6972C34 2002   jC813'.54   C2001-911725-6

PZ7.B969Ca 2002

First published in the United States, 2002

Library of Congress Catalog Card Number: 20011099126

Orca Book Publishers gratefully acknowledges the support for our publishing programs provided by the following agencies: The Government of Canada through the Book Publishing Industry Development Program (BPIDP), The Canada Council for the Arts, and the British Columbia Arts Council.

Design: Christine Toller
Cover illustration: Ljuba Levstek
Printed and bound in Canada

IN CANADA:
Orca Book Publishers
PO Box 5626, Station B
Victoria, BC Canada
V8R 6S4

IN THE UNITED STATES:
Orca Book Publishers
PO Box 468
Custer, WA USA
98240-0468

04 03 02 • 5 4 3 2 1

For Cole and Gramps with Big, Big love

KB

CHAPTER 1

I swear on my baseball glove — Kelly and I had nothing to do with that fire.

Oh, sure, we were there. I'm not denying that. But we didn't start the fire. As a matter of fact, we were the ones who put it out and cleaned up the mess. But did nosy old Mrs. Butterman see *that* from her kitchen window?

It wasn't even a real fire anyway — just Craig Leskiew getting rid of his math test so his parents wouldn't find out he'd flunked it. The flames probably would have died down in a few seconds — it wasn't that big a test — but Billy Thompson and the other guys decided to pile on candy wrappers and Popsicle sticks, and that gave the fire a bit more life. Even so, it still would've gone out if it hadn't been so close to the wooden climbing frame. It was a total accident how those flames jumped onto the post.

That's when everybody got scared and took off. And since Kelly and I were the only ones left, we put the fire out. No big deal. We doused it with our Slurpies. Then we scooped up the ashes and dumped them into the trash. End of story.

At least, it should have been. But no. Old *let's-see-how-much-trouble-I-can-cause* Butterman has to call the fire department and the newspaper and the school board and everybody else she can think of. So for the rest of the evening, mobs of people were hanging around the schoolyard, staring at the charred post of the play structure. That little fire got a better turnout than the community barbecue.

That's why I wasn't too surprised when Kelly and I got hauled into the principal's office the next morning.

Mrs. MacDonald's long red fingernails rat-a-tatted on the desktop as she made a big show of studying some official-looking paper. Every now and again she'd frown at us over the top of her glasses, shake her head and then look back at the paper. Finally she sat back in her chair and said, "Now — would you boys like to tell me about last night's little fire?"

Kelly slouched in his chair. "Not really."

Mrs. MacDonald lowered her head like a bull about to charge.

"That was a rhetorical question, Kelly," she said. "It does not require an answer."

"Does that mean we *don't* have to tell you about

the fire?" I piped up.

Mrs. MacDonald upgraded her frown to a glare. "No, Michael. That isn't what it means."

"But you said —"

Mrs. MacDonald closed her eyes and sort of breathed through her teeth.

"Never mind what I said. Tell me about the fire."

Kelly shrugged. "There's nothing to tell."

"Let me be the judge of that," Mrs. MacDonald told him.

Kelly picked up a framed photograph off her desk.

"Are these your kids?" he asked.

Mrs. MacDonald took the photograph from him and set it back down.

"Could we stick to the topic, please? Did you boys start last night's fire?"

"No," Kelly and I answered at the same time.

"That's not what Mrs. Butterman says."

When I heard that, I almost flew out of my chair. Kelly just shook his head and looked out the window.

"Whatever," he muttered under his breath.

I didn't understand how he could be so calm, considering Mrs. Butterman was trying to get us in trouble — *again*!

Ever since that time we used the green tomatoes in her garden for batting practice, she's had it in for us. Okay — I admit we shouldn't have helped ourselves, but I'm pretty sure she wouldn't have given them to us if we'd asked. And thanks to those tomatoes, Kelly and I both hit home runs in the championship game. Mrs. Butterman should have been glad to help. Instead, she sicked the police on us before we'd even finished celebrating our victory. Naturally, the cops made us pay for the tomatoes and apologize for what we'd done, but that wasn't enough for Mrs. Butterman. She wanted us thrown in jail!

And if people got to thinking Kelly and I were the ones who'd started that fire, she might get her wish.

"Mrs. Butterman is lying!" I blurted.

"Oh, really?" The tone of Mrs. MacDonald's voice said she didn't believe me. "And why would she do that, Michael? Mrs. Butterman is secretary-treasurer of Calumet Park Community Center, as well as president of the Friendship Circle Ladies' Auxiliary. That's the group who raised the money for the play structure that *someone* tried to burn down last night. Mrs. Butterman is also a Block Parent, she's a volunteer in the school's Reading Recovery program, and her home is a designated evacuation site in the event of a school emergency."

Then Mrs. MacDonald pulled a couple of file folders toward her. One was thicker than the other, but they were both pretty fat. She opened them. "You boys — on the other hand — have accumulated a somewhat *different* list of accomplishments. In this school year alone you have been kept for detention by your teachers no less than fifty-five times."

"That's both of us together," I pointed out. Divided

by two that was only twenty-seven and a half detentions in nine months. I didn't want things seeming worse than they were.

Mrs. MacDonald lowered the paper she was reading and sent me her best glare.

I sat back in my chair and closed my mouth.

She continued leafing through the folders. "According to my records, you two were the masterminds behind the infamous synchronized book drop that shook the school last November. The superintendent was in our building that day, and he thought we were experiencing an earthquake. If I'm not mistaken — and I'm *not*," her voice suddenly reminded me of concrete, "February's giant snowmen were your creations as well. While the Parent Advisory Committee was holding its monthly meeting, you boys built huge snowmen in front of all the school exits so that no one could get out of the building."

Kelly and I exchanged smirks as Mrs. MacDonald flipped the page.

"Oh, yes — and then there was this little gem." She waved a newspaper clipping at us. "This one earned the school a write-up in the paper. It was the morning of our Easter assembly. I trust you recall the occasion. Everyone in the auditorium — students, teachers, parents, school board guests — had risen for the playing of the national anthem. Do you remember? But instead of 'O Canada', we were all treated to 'Old MacDonald Had A Farm.' "

Something about the way Mrs. MacDonald gritted her teeth as she spoke told me she hadn't found that joke particularly funny. She took off her glasses so that we would get the full effect of her scowl. Then she said, "Need I continue?"

I glanced at the folders on her desk. She'd barely made a dent. At the rate she was going, we'd be in her office all day.

"No, that's okay," I told her.

Kelly nudged me. "I think that's another one of those rhetorical questions, Midge," he said. Then he turned to Mrs. MacDonald and grinned. "Right?"

It's tough to say which was redder, Mrs. MacDonald's fingernails or her face.

"You do a good deed, and this is the thanks you get," I grumbled as Kelly and I trudged around the schoolyard in the pouring rain, collecting garbage. "A whole month of picking up other people's soggy sandwich crusts and used tissues — *yuck*! We should've let the play structure burn down."

Kelly shrugged. "Don't sweat it. So we have to pick up a little garbage. At least we're outside."

I turned my face to the sky and squinted into the rain. "Yeah — getting soaked!"

"Think of it as liquid sunshine," he said.

My nose was dripping rain like a leaky faucet. I took a swipe at it and frowned. "Why are you being so cool about this? We're being punished for something we didn't do. Doesn't that bother you even a little?"

Kelly grinned. "Not when I think about all the stuff we *haven't* been punished for."

"Speak for yourself," I groused as I stuffed a crumpled cardboard cup into the garbage bag. "I've never gotten away with anything in my life. I can't even drop a crumb on the floor without sirens going off. And last night my folks said that if they get even one more phone call from Mrs. MacDonald, they're going to put me in a private school!"

Kelly prodded a partially eaten apple with his shoe and then stepped over it. "Could be worse."

"How do you figure?"

"They could've yanked you off the baseball team."

CHAPTER 2

As we took the field for our warm-up the next night, I thought about what Kelly had said. But it didn't worry me. You see, my parents have never threatened to take me out of baseball. It's not that they're softhearted or anything. It's just that baseball is the one place I don't get into trouble, so why would they mess with a good thing?

The coach started hitting grounders. I scooped up a short hopper, touched first and fired the ball home. Then I glanced into the stands.

They were crammed full, and there were lawn chairs strung along both baselines for the overflow. Other teams are lucky to get that kind of turnout for the playoffs, but it's a regular thing for us.

My dad was parked in his normal spot behind home plate. He's president of the Umpires' Association, and when he's not officiating, he likes to call the game from the stands. That drives my mom crazy, so she sits somewhere else — usually as far away from my dad as she can get. Today she was at the top of the bleachers beside Kelly's mom.

She and Ms. Romani almost always sit together. They don't talk — they just sit together. It's my mom's way of including Ms. Romani in the community. You see, except for baseball games, Kelly's mom is pretty much a loner. She doesn't speak English very well, so that might have something to do with it. But I have a feeling the real reason she has no friends is because Kelly's her son.

The ball came at me again. I whipped it to second, hustled over to first and waited for the return throw.

If infield practice meant anything, we were going to have a good game. Of course, Kelly was pitching, so that pretty much cinched it anyway. In the past three seasons, we haven't lost once when he's been on the mound.

He's unbeatable. He's got a nasty curve ball and a mean change-up, but his killer pitch is his fastball — I haven't hit it yet!

At the end of last season, the league got hold of one of those speed guns they use in the majors, and Kelly's fastball clocked in at seventy miles an hour. *Seventy miles an hour!* Batters can't even see the ball at that speed, never mind hit it! And Kelly's only thirteen. I can't wait to see what his fastball will be like in a couple more years.

When he isn't pitching, Kelly plays center field. It's not that we don't have other guys to play that position, but Kelly's just too good to leave on the bench. Not only does he hit like Mark McGwire, but he can run the bases, turn double plays and make catches that just shouldn't be made. My dad says it takes nine guys to field a team, but maybe it would only take three if they could all play like Kelly. Everybody knows he's the reason the stands are always full.

Away from the ballpark, it's a different story. Teachers don't want Kelly in their classrooms, storekeepers don't want him in their shops, and parents don't want him in their homes. They all think he's trouble. But come game time, those same people pour into the stands to see Kelly play ball.

It's so weird. They love him and hate him at the same time — adults, that is. Kids don't have that problem. They like Kelly just fine. Come to think of it, that's probably why grown-ups don't.

You see, Kelly's a magnet, except that instead of iron filings sticking to him, it's kids. They follow him everywhere. You'd almost think he was the Pied Piper. And he doesn't even work at it. He's just one of those people with charisma.

He's taller than most guys our age and more muscular too. So right away he stands out from everybody else. Then there are his looks. According to Deenie Jamieson, Kelly is tall, dark, and handsomewith a smile to die for. I don't know about that, but he does have a big smile — and he smiles a lot.

That's another thing that irritates adults. They can yell at him from morning 'til night, but all they'll get is high blood pressure — and a smile. Naturally, that earns Kelly the respect of every kid in the school. They'd love to be as cool as he is, but let a grown-up start chewing them out, and they're whining in no time.

Maybe the reason Kelly doesn't get rattled is because he's had so much experience. I'm not saying he goes looking for trouble. Neither of us does. It's more like *it* finds *us*. And really — most of the time — grown-ups are the ones to blame. They're always telling us to use our heads, and then when we do, they have a fit.

Take the time we wanted to go to the movies but didn't have the money. We could've sneaked into the show, but we didn't even consider it. Instead, we sat down outside the theater to figure out a way to get the admission. All Kelly did was put his hat on the sidewalk while he was thinking. It was a total surprise when a lady walked by and dropped fifty cents into it. So he just left it there and, before we knew it, we had enough money for the show *and* popcorn.

It worked out great. At least, it would have if Mrs. Butterman hadn't seen us and phoned my parents. I swear that woman knows my number better than her own! And then, because my mother had never been so mortified in her life — whatever that means — I got grounded for a week!

Not Kelly, though. In fact, Mrs. Butterman didn't even bother calling his place. Between Kelly's smile and his mom's bad English, she must have known she wouldn't win.

The coach bunted the ball along the baseline, and I tore off to get it. Then I flipped it to Barry Martin, who had come over to cover the bag.

"Okay," the coach hollered. "Bring it in, fellas."

"Who's umping tonight, Midge?" one of the guys asked as we filed into the dugout.

In my mind I tried to picture the officiating schedule on the fridge at home. "I think Hollings is on the bases," I said.

"What about behind the plate?"

"The Mann," I gurgled through a gulp of water.

The Mann is everybody's favorite ump. He's the best. He's honest and he's fair, and there isn't anything he doesn't know about baseball. He has so many stats crammed into his head you'd think he was a computer. I'm not exaggerating. Before every game, somebody tries to stump him with a baseball trivia question — it's sort of become a tradition — but he always has the answer. *Always*! He's a baseball genius.

"I got him beat tonight," Jerry Fletcher announced, hauling a crumpled scrap of paper from his pocket.

"Bet you don't," Kelly said, sliding onto the bench.

"Oh, yeah. I do," Jerry insisted. "Just wait 'til

you hear the question."

"Shoot," someone else said.

"Okay." Jerry squinted at the paper. "Who is the only major league player to steal five bases in a single game?"

"What's so hard about that?" Barry said.

"Do you know the answer?"

"I could probably guess."

Jerry crossed his arms over his chest. "Fine. Guess away."

Barry thought for a couple of seconds before answering. "Lou Brock."

"Wrong."

I gave it a shot. "Ricky Henderson?"

"Wrong."

"How about Ron LeFlore?" Pete Jacobs took a stab at it too. If anybody were going to get the right answer, it would be him.

"Wrong," Jerry gloated.

"So who is it?"

Jerry glanced toward home, where the Mann was brushing off the plate. He lowered his voice. "Tony Gwynn."

"Get outta here," Pete said. "Gwynn wasn't a base stealer."

Jerry grinned. "That's why it's such a good question. Even the Mann won't get this one."

"Fifty cents says he does," Kelly dared him.

Jerry came back to the dugout frowning. He chucked a couple of quarters at Kelly and flopped onto the bench.

"That's the easiest money I ever made," Kelly grinned.

"Shut up," said Jerry.

"Play ball," said the Mann.

CHAPTER 3

"Now batting for the Calumet Park Rebels, wearing number seventeen, the pitcher — Cairo Kelly Romani!"

Whoops and whistles erupted from the stands as Kelly made his way to the batter's box. He touched the far side of the plate with his bat and pawed the dirt a few times as he settled into his batting stance. Then he took a couple of practice swings.

I slid a weight onto my bat and stepped into the on-deck circle. The game was tied at three and there were two outs, but we had runners at the corners. With only one inning left, the other team couldn't afford to let us score. If they were smart, they'd walk Kelly and pitch to me.

They did. The only problem — for them — is that I hit a line drive right through the middle, scoring two — and that was enough to win the game.

Back in the dugout, my team congratulated me.

"Way to come through, Midge."

That's me. Midge is my nickname. My real name is Michael — Michael Ridge — but somebody called me Midge one day, and it stuck. Now everybody calls me that — except for my teachers and Mrs. Butterman. I suppose when I grow up and become a lawyer or an accountant or something like that, I might want to be called Michael, but for now, Midge is fine.

Kelly has a nickname too, but he gave it to himself — Cairo Kelly. The Kelly part he got from his mom; the Cairo bit was his idea. It's his way of remembering his dad — well, maybe not remembering, him exactly, since he never knew him in the first place, but adding Cairo lets everybody know he had a dad.

You see, Ms. Romani never got married. Kelly says she was going to, but the Egyptian sailor she was in love with got killed in a shipwreck before their wedding day. And because his parents never actually made it to the altar, Kelly couldn't take his dad's last name. So he did the next best thing. He added Cairo to the beginning — on account of his dad being Egyptian and all.

Anyway, it sounds pretty cool when the public address guy says it over the loudspeaker at baseball games, and I wouldn't be surprised if it stays with Kelly all the way to the big leagues.

When I stop to think about it, I guess there are

lots of people with nicknames. Take the Mann, for instance. Now there's a good nickname. In fact, I bet there aren't more than a half dozen guys in our baseball league who even know what the Mann's real name is. I do, but that's because it's on my dad's umpire list at home. It's also on the staff list at my school — not something most kids get a look at, but then, most kids don't spend as much time in the office as I do.

The Mann is really Harold Mann — quiet, middle-aged Harold Mann, custodian at Calumet Park Middle School. From eight until four, he is the sweeper-upper of spitballs, screwer-inner of light bulbs, and painter-over of graffiti. And he is invisible. Well, not really, but he's so quiet, no one notices him. He's just part of the school, like the chalkboards and the desks.

But as soon as he puts on his umpire's uniform and steps onto the baseball field, he turns into a completely different person. Harold Mann, the janitor, disappears, and the Mann takes his place. And he really is "the man." I don't know what it is, but there's something about him that says he's in control, and somehow that puts everybody at ease. It's like as long as the Mann is running the show, people are sure it will go smooth. And it always does.

After the game, the coach asked Kelly and me to collect the bats and helmets and put them in his van, so by the time we got to the concession for our complementary post-game drinks, every guy on both teams was ahead of us.

Kelly grabbed his throat and started gasping.

"I ain't gonna make it," he croaked, letting his knees buckle under him. "I'm dyin' of thirst. I need … root beer."

Then he became a dead weight on my shoulder, and *my* knees almost buckled.

"You're supposed to cry for *water*, not root beer, you moron," I said, pushing him off me.

"You can have my root beer, Kelly," a girl's voice slithered over my shoulder.

I turned to look. It was Babe Ruth — not *the* Babe Ruth, but Ruth Robertson. Us guys just call her Babe because she's good-looking. Anyway, Ruth was standing right behind me, fluttering blue eyelashes and holding out her drink to Kelly. I shook my head. Ruth's been chasing Kelly for months. So far he's barely noticed her, though. But then, why would he? It's baseball season!

"Pitching looks like really hard work," Ruth purred. "You must be thirsty as anything."

"*I* am!" I said, making a grab for the can of pop.

Ruth glared at me and pulled the drink away. Then her face got all soft again as she turned back to Kelly.

"That was a great game, Kelly. You were awesome." She gave him a come-on smile, then lowered her eyes and added, "Are you that good at *everything*?" Pause. "Or just pitching?"

Ruth was putting out more electricity than a power plant, but if Kelly was feeling the zap, it didn't show. He just smiled his easy smile and reached for the root beer.

"Thanks, Ruth." Then he held out his drink coupon to her. "Here. Get yourself a replacement."

Ruth shook her head.

"You keep it. I'm not that thirsty."

"You sure?"

"Mmm-hmm."

"Well, okay — if you're positive." Another smile. "Thanks again."

Then Kelly chugged the drink and handed Ruth back the empty can. Her eyes went all dreamy, and I wondered what she would have done if he'd handed her a million bucks.

But I didn't have long to think about it, because just then our coach, Mr. Bryant, came jogging toward us. He had this intense look on his face, so — of course — my first thought was that we were in trouble. I tried to remember if we'd left any bats in the dugout or locked his keys in the van. But when the coach planted himself between Ruth and Kelly, I decided he just didn't want girls getting in the way of Kelly and baseball.

Mr. Bryant put his hand on Kelly's shoulder and pointed toward the diamond. The Mann was still at home plate, talking with some guy I didn't recognize.

"You see that fella standing with the ump?" the coach said.

Kelly nodded. "Yeah."

"You know who he is?"

Kelly squinted and then shook his head. "Nope. I've never seen him before."

"Well, I bet you've read his stuff," the coach said. "That's Skylar Hogue, head writer for *Sport Beat* magazine, and he wants to do a story on you!" the coach practically shouted.

Kelly's face split into a grin. "No kidding?"

The coach stabbed a knuckle into Kelly's chest. "This could be the break of a lifetime, Romani!"

Kelly kept smiling, so the coach kept talking.

"Everybody in sports knows Skylar Hogue. He rubs elbows with professional athletes every single day — and he wants an interview with *you*. With *you*, Romani — *you*, a teeny-bop pitcher on a community baseball team. Beats me how he even knows you exist, but don't look a gift horse in the mouth — that's what I always say. And this is one big gift horse! The guy's got connections all over the place. If he decides you're something special, it could open the door to the majors for you!"

Kelly grinned. "Cool."

"Cool?" The coach yanked Kelly's cap over his eyes. "Is that all you can say? The opportunity of a lifetime is staring you in the face, and all you can say is *cool*? I'm telling you, kid — if you blow this, you'll be kicking yourself for the rest of your life. So be smart. Nobody likes a wise guy. Remember that. Be polite. Be respectful.

Just answer the man's questions as …"

And that's all I caught, because Kelly and the coach were already halfway to the diamond.

CHAPTER 4

The morning after *Sport Beat* magazine came out, there were so many copies of it in the school, you would've thought it was a textbook. Even our social studies teacher had one, and when he pulled it out during third period, I felt like I'd won the lottery. You see, I hadn't done my homework, and I was pretty sure Mr. Mayes wasn't going to believe that thieves had broken into my house during the night and stolen it. So when he started reading Skylar Hogue's column out loud, I was his best listener.

In the article, Hogue talked about watching Kelly pitch, and how it was hard to believe he was only thirteen. *As good as I've seen for one so young* — those were his exact words. He also said that with the right opportunities, Kelly had a real chance of playing professional ball someday. Then he mentioned meeting Kelly after the game, and described him as *a pleasant young man with his head screwed on straight*. That could only mean Kelly had followed the coach's advice and held off on the wisecracks.

When Mr. Mayes was nearly finished reading, I noticed the Mann sweeping the hallway outside the classroom, and I wondered what *he'd* thought of the article. I tried to read his face, but it didn't tell me a thing. In fact, he didn't even look like he'd been listening — though how he could miss Mr. Mayes' voice blaring through the open door is a mystery to me.

On the way to our next class, I saw the Mann again. Too bad Kelly didn't. He was so busy auto-graphing magazines, he walked right into the back of him.

"Oops. Sorry," he apologized, and then, when he realized who he'd smacked into, he waved the magazine and beamed, "Did you see the story about me? Pretty good, eh?"

But all the Mann said was, "Actions speak louder than words, my boy."

Kelly's mom wasn't all that impressed with the article either. Mind you, Kelly didn't pick the best time to show it to her — even I could see that.

It was after school, and we were at his place, looking at his new Carlos Delgado poster. I'd only planned to stay a few minutes, but one thing led to another, and somehow I never left. So when his mom came in from work, we were both sprawled on the couch in the living room, watching television and munching on Doritos.

It's funny how you can be looking at something but not really seeing it until somebody else does. That's how it was when Kelly's mom walked into the apartment. The second before she opened the door, the living room had been real comfortable, but as soon as she came into it, the coziness evaporated, and all I could see was the mess. The coffee table was covered with broken chips and wet rings from our drinks. Kelly's poster collection and the cushions that had been lined up along the back of the couch when we'd arrived were all over the floor, and there were more Doritos mashed into the carpet. I can't honestly say I noticed the crucifix hanging crooked on the wall, but Ms. Romani did and, without even putting down her grocery bags, she walked over and straightened it.

"Hi, Ma." Kelly punched the off button on the remote and stood up. Then he took the groceries from his mom and headed for the kitchen. "What's for dinner?"

Ms. Romani sighed, her shoulders collapsed, and her raincoat slid down her arms and into her hands. Underneath, she was wearing a way-too-pink maid's uniform that made me wish I'd brought my sunglasses. She trudged into the hallway and draped her coat over a pile of others already on a wall hook. Then she came back into the living room and began picking the cushions up off the floor.

"Hello, Meej," she said with a half-smile that seemed to take more energy than she had.

"Hey, Ms. Romani," I said back, jumping off the couch to help clean up the mess. "Tough day at the hotel?"

She shrugged and started gathering up the posters.

"Not so good, but not so bad too."

"*Either*, Ma." Kelly came back into the room, munching an apple. "Not so bad *either*."

Ms. Romani stood up.

"Not so bad *either*," she said, glaring at Kelly and pushing the posters into his arms. "How come you can correct my talking, but you can't pick up for yourself?"

"I was gonna do it, Ma," Kelly protested. "Honest."

"Sure, sure," she muttered, scraping at the chip crumbs on the rug.

"No, Ma. Really, I was. You just got home sooner than I expected."

"I'm always home at the same time."

Kelly opened his mouth and closed it again. "You're right," he conceded. "You're right, Ma. I'm just making excuses because I don't want you to be mad at me — " then he grinned this huge grin " — *not today*."

Ms. Romani peered up at him for a second and then went back to scrubbing at the carpet. I guess she was immune to Kelly's smile.

"Don't you want to know why today's special, Ma?" Kelly was still grinning.

"No," Ms. Romani said, and this time she didn't even look up.

But Kelly wasn't fazed. He dumped the posters onto a chair and began dragging his mom to her feet.

"Yes, you do."

Ms. Romani made a feeble attempt to twist away.

"Kelly!" she complained, but the way she said it, it sounded more like Kaylie. All Ms. Romani's e's sound like a's, and her i's sound like e's.

"C'mon, Ma," Kelly laughed, depositing her on the couch and flopping down beside her. "I want you to look at this." He picked the *Sport Beat* magazine off the table and waved it at her.

Ms. Romani must've realized she wasn't going to win, because she stopped struggling and sank back against the cushions. Then she muttered something in Italian. Finally, she lifted her hands in the air and grumbled, "So show me already."

Kelly flipped to Skylar Hogue's article and plunked the magazine into his mother's lap.

She leaned forward and peered at the photograph of Kelly grinning at her from the page. Then she looked at the real thing grinning beside her.

"What's this?" she asked, pointing at the magazine.

"It's me, Ma. Don't you recognize your own son?" Kelly teased.

Ms. Romani went to cuff him, but he ducked out of reach, and she turned back to the magazine. Then she announced, "You need a haircut."

Kelly rolled his eyes, but said nothing.

She studied the magazine for a few more seconds and then demanded, "How come your picture is here?"

Kelly swelled up his chest and struck a pose. "Because I'm a star," he said.

Ms. Romani snorted and went to cuff him again. This time she didn't miss.

"Ow!" Kelly grumbled and rubbed his ear. "Why'd you do that?"

"You want stars? I give you stars," she said, and I had to bite the inside of my bottom lip to keep from laughing. For someone who didn't speak English very well, that was a pretty good line. "So, Mister *Star*, tell me how come you're in a magazine."

"Because Skylar Hogue is an important sportswriter, and he thinks I can play in the big leagues someday. So he wrote an article about me. Do you know what that means, Ma?"

Ms. Romani scowled and her arms started waving like propeller blades.

"What do you mean, do I know what it means? I'm your mother. Sure, I know what it means. It means your head is gonna get big with dreams that aren't gonna happen."

Kelly sighed. "It means there's a chance that I can play professional ball one day." He shook the magazine at her. "This is *Sport Beat*. Everybody who's anybody in the sports world reads this magazine. And they're gonna be reading about me. About *me*, Ma! They're gonna know I'm alive, and they're gonna be keeping their eyes on me. All I have to do is play baseball."

Ms. Romani sprang up off the couch.

"Baseball, baseball, baseball. That's all you think about."

Kelly jumped up too.

"What's wrong with that? I love baseball. And I'm good at it." He shook the magazine again. "Obviously other people think so too!"

"And these other people — are they gonna feed you when you don't get your dream? When you don't get your school, and you aren't the big shot baseball player, then what? I'll tell you what! You'll be sweeping Mr. Tonelli's butcher shop!"

The discussion was getting louder by the second, and even though I'd have had to be totally deaf not to hear what they were saying, I suddenly felt like an eavesdropper. I began sidestepping my way toward the door.

I cleared my throat. "Well, I guess I should get going," I said as casually as I could. "It's getting close to supper."

But neither Kelly nor his mom even looked at me, and I began to wonder if I'd become invisible.

"I won't be sweeping for Mr. Tonelli or anybody else, Ma — not ever! And you want to know why?

Because someday I'm going to be somebody! Baseball is gonna make me somebody important. And then no one will ever put me — or you — down again!"

More loud Italian and more arm waving.

"Why can't you have a little faith in me?" Kelly shouted back. "Don't you want me to succeed?"

I turned the door handle and waved. "Goodbye, Ms. Romani."

No answer.

"See you at school tomorrow, Kelly."

But the two of them were so caught up in their argument, I could've run off with the television, and they wouldn't have noticed.

CHAPTER 5

As the playoffs came closer, Kelly's game got better and better. Maybe he was inspired by Skylar Hogue's article, or maybe he just wanted to prove something to his mom. All I know is that he was totally focused on baseball — which was great for the team, but not so good for the other parts of Kelly's life.

Like school, for instance. Kelly's body kept coming to class, but his brain wasn't with it. Neither were his books or his homework. Half the time he didn't even bring anything to write with. And he didn't pay the slightest attention to the lessons either, so when he got called on, he had no clue what question was being asked — never mind what the answer was. Teachers aren't real patient with Kelly at the best of times, so it wasn't long before he was spending most of his days in the hall and office.

I couldn't understand it. Kelly's no dummy, and though he's never been much for schoolwork, he's always squeaked by on his natural smarts and what he takes in through his skin. But suddenly nothing was working. I'm not saying it wouldn't have if Kelly had made some kind of effort, but he didn't. There were no con jobs, no excuses, no stalling — nothing. He didn't even try to *smile* his way out of trouble. Driving teachers crazy has always been a game with Kelly, but suddenly he just didn't seem to care.

So it wasn't exactly a shock when he got suspended. It was just a matter of time — even without what happened in Miss Drummond's class. The thing is, the rest of us should have been suspended right along with him.

Miss Drummond is our English teacher. She is also the school drama coach — *and* she is weird. I don't know if it's the thirty-plus years of teaching drama that's warped her, or if she's always been a little strange, and drama is just a good fit. It doesn't really matter. The point is she's weird. To Miss Drummond, life is one big play — starring her. It shows in everything about her, from her facial expressions and the clothes she wears to the way she walks and the things that come out of her mouth. So, of course, no one takes her seriously.

As crazy as she is, though, I can't help feeling a little sorry for her. Kids are always laughing at her behind her back — she just doesn't know it. To make matters worse, she has acne. Miss Drummond has to be at least fifty years old, but she has worse acne than any kid in the school. And that's why Kelly got suspended. That, and the fact that it was Thursday.

English with Miss Drummond is never wonderful, but on Thursdays it's downright painful. That's because there's no drama on Thursdays — no drama classes, no drama club meetings, no play rehearsals, no drama of any kind. And since Miss Drummond is addicted to drama, Thursdays sort of throw her into an artsy version of withdrawal.

When smokers go into withdrawal, they search ashtrays for cigarette butts. Miss Drummond turns her English classes into Shakespearean festivals.

On this particular Thursday, the theme was readers' theater, which — as far as I'm concerned — is right up there with being sat on by a sumo wrestler — it hurts, but you don't usually die from it. Anyway, for the first ten minutes of the period, Miss Drummond was flitting through the classroom with her bracelets jangling and her filmy dress wafting around her like line-dried laundry on a windy day, arranging us into what she called performing pods. Basically what that meant was that we were in groups for choral reading. There were some kids who had solo parts, though, and Kelly was one of them.

"I can't do it. I don't have my book," Kelly told Miss Drummond when she tried to move him into position.

Miss Drummond made a tut-tutting sound and floated over to the bookshelf. "I am powerless to comprehend what has come over you of late, Mr. Romani," she said as she handed him a book. "I do believe you'd forget your head were it not attached."

"Nice try, Kel," I hissed when she'd turned away.

Miss Drummond spun around so fast her dress flared like a parachute opening up.

"Who said that?" she demanded, jamming her hands onto her hips and glaring around the room. Her gaze came to rest on Barry Martin, who was standing beside me. "Are you the source of that utterance, Mr. Martin?" she frowned at him.

Barry's cheeks instantly turned purple, and even though he shook his head, he was the picture of guilt.

She walked right up to him and wagged her finger under his nose, setting all her bracelets jangling again. "Don't flaunt falsehoods at me, young man." Her painted-on eyebrows kind of quivered. "Do you imagine I have toiled in the field of pedagogy these many years without acquiring the ability to discern when I am being led up the garden path, as it were?"

"Yes, ma'am," Barry mumbled apologetically, and then when Miss Drummond's gasp told him he'd said the wrong thing, his cheeks went purpler than ever and he sputtered, "I mean — no! No, ma'am. I didn't. I mean — I don't. Honest!"

Miss Drummond is a sucker for groveling. Her

face relaxed. "Perhaps I misheard," she conceded. Then she was all smiles again as she clapped her hands and said, "All right. Places, everyone. Mr. Romani, you stand over here behind the flip chart." She rolled it into position. "For our purposes today, you will have to imagine it is an arras, and that you, our Hamlet, are concealed behind it. Keep in mind that — "

"Excuse me, Miss Drummond," Alicia Wagoner interrupted. She was probably the only kid in class who actually liked Thursday English, but then she was also the only kid in class who belonged to Miss Drummond's drama club.

"Yes, my dear." Miss Drummond flashed Alicia a brilliant smile. All Miss Drummond's back teeth are gold, and when they catch the fluorescent lights, they glint like crazy.

"What exactly is an arras, Miss Drummond?" Alicia asked.

"That's an excellent question, Alicia," Miss Drummond beamed. "How astute of you to recognize that others in the class might not be familiar with the term. It has, after all, become more or less obsolete. But in the era of the bard ..." She stressed the word bard, paused and then smiled as if it was some kind of inside joke. Alicia was the only one who smiled back. "Well, suffice it to say that during the Elizabethan period, the word was commonplace. An arras was a heavy tapestry used as a wall hanging. And since the castles of the time tended to be drafty domiciles, an arras provided not only a pleasing diversion for the eye, but also insulation against the cold."

I scratched my head. I didn't have the faintest idea what she'd just said. "Has she answered the question yet?" I whispered to Barry Martin.

"Shut up," he growled back, obviously still ticked off at getting in trouble because of me.

But either the room was too quiet or Barry was too loud, because Miss Drummond instantly whirled on him.

"How dare you!" she huffed indignantly.

"I didn't mean *you*, Miss Drummond," Barry said quickly, once again turning the color of someone being strangled.

But Miss Drummond wasn't about to listen to him a second time. She pointed to the door. "Out."

"But I —"

"Out!" Her voice rose an octave, and she stamped her foot. "Out, out, out!"

As Barry made his way toward the exit, Kelly pushed the flip chart toward him.

"Wanna hide behind my arras?" he snickered.

Barry sent him a dirty look and stepped out of the way. So the flip chart kept right on rolling — until it smacked into the chalkboard and went crashing to the floor.

The room suddenly became very quiet, and Miss Drummond's mouth dropped open. Then it closed. Then it opened again.

Kelly walked over to the fallen flip chart, stared down at it for a few seconds and shook his head. Then he turned to Miss Drummond and shrugged. "They just don't make arrases like they used to."

That's when the whole class burst out laughing. Okay, maybe not everyone. Alicia Wagoner didn't laugh, and Barry Martin didn't dare laugh, but the rest of us thought the situation was pretty funny. At least, we did until Miss Drummond began screeching.

"Stop it! Stop it, stop it, stop it!" she shrieked, shaking her head so violently that a barrette jumped out of her hair and bounced across the floor. She didn't even notice.

"Don't have a cow, Miss Drummond," Kelly said, righting the flip chart. "It was only a joke."

That was the wrong thing to say.

Miss Drummond was instantly in Kelly's face.

"This is not humorous, Mr. Romani! It is a great many things, but humorous is not among them. It is disruptive, and it is definitely disrespectful, but it is *not* humorous!"

Then she turned on the entire class. "Be quiet, all of you!" she shouted. "I try to make classes provocative and meaningful, and this is the thanks I get! You resist all attempts at enlightenment. You take any and every opportunity to impugn me and each other. Why ... why ... why, you are nothing more than an unwieldy rabble of cretins!"

Everyone had been inching in from the different

parts of the room as she was speaking, so we were all huddled together in front of her now.

Miss Drummond's eyes flashed with anger, and little beads of perspiration popped out on her upper lip. Whatever it was she'd just said, she obviously meant it.

And she wasn't finished.

"Well, I shall not tolerate it one second longer! Do you hear me?" she cried. "I have half a mind to call all your parents!"

Kelly nudged me and whispered, "I wonder what happened to the other half of her mind." But something about the way the room suddenly got really quiet told me I wasn't the only one who'd heard him.

I looked at Miss Drummond. Her body was rigid and trembling, and she was breathing in snorts. Then her face turned bright red, and the zits on it started to pulse.

She stood like that for so long, I began to wonder if she was having a stroke. And then, with every eye in the class glued to her face, the unthinkable happened.

The huge, shiny white pimple in the middle of Miss Drummond's chin popped.

CHAPTER 6

Miss Drummond and Kelly both missed the next two days of school. Miss Drummond was suffering from a migraine; Kelly was suffering from a suspension. And he wasn't very happy about it.

In fact, at baseball practice on Friday, he was as grouchy as I've ever seen him. It was a nice evening, sunny and warm, but you'd never have known it by looking at Kelly. He was walking around under his own personal thundercloud. His pitching was even off.

You didn't need to be a mind reader to see that something was bugging him. I figured his mom was probably on his case about the suspension. I know mine would have been. But since Kelly didn't seem real anxious to talk about it, I didn't ask. I did ask him if he wanted to go to a movie the next day, but he said he had something else to do.

The day after that was Sunday. I never see Kelly on Sundays unless we have a game. That's because he has church, and then he and his mom take a bus to the next town to visit his grandpa, who lives in a nursing home there. And since Kelly was still suspended on Monday, I didn't see him again until Tuesday.

English was our first class that morning, and because it was also the first time Kelly and Miss Drummond had faced each other since the zit incident, I was semi-prepared for more fireworks. But there weren't any. In fact, the class was pretty dull. Miss Drummond must still have been mad at us, because she wasn't the least bit creative. Neither was Kelly. In fact, he was a model student — had his books and everything. He even put his hand up to answer a few questions. It was obvious he'd turned over a new leaf, because he stayed that way the whole day, even when we took to the field after school to collect garbage.

I scanned the grounds and shook my head. Kelly and I had been cleaning the schoolyard every day for three weeks, but it never seemed to run out of garbage. I was beginning to wonder if Mrs. MacDonald had hired somebody to litter it up just for us.

"How come you're in such a good mood today?" I asked, stuffing the remains of someone's exploded notebook into the black plastic bag.

"What do you mean? I'm always in a good mood," Kelly said.

I glanced at him sideways and snorted. "Right

— and that snarly face you were wearing at Friday's practice is your new smile," I said sarcastically.

He looked a bit embarrassed. "So I had an off-day. I'm entitled."

I couldn't argue with that. I mean, nobody's happy every single minute — not even Kelly. And it's not like he didn't have a reason to be grumpy. Anyway, he was back to his normal self again, so what did it matter?

I let the subject drop, and scooped up a brown lunch bag and a crumpled wad of waxed paper. Kelly headed for something that looked like tinfoil. After three weeks of garbage duty, we'd come up with a pretty good system. First we'd do a zigzag sweep of the field, picking trash up along the way, and then we'd walk around the fence to snag the stuff blown there by the wind. After that, all we had to do was turn in our garbage bag to the Mann, so he could let Mrs. MacDonald know we hadn't skipped out.

When we'd started that day, the Mann had been trimming the hedges at the front of the school, so that's where we headed when we were done.

"It's hard to believe there are only two more games before playoffs," Kelly said as he chucked a stone the length of the field. "The Barons tonight and then the Lightning on Thursday. If Bartlett is pitching for the Barons, it should be a pretty good game."

I nodded. Freddie Bartlett wasn't anywhere near as good as Kelly, but he could still strike you out.

Kelly threw another stone. "Is the Mann umping tonight?"

"Yeah," I said, "but not behind the plate."

"Too bad. What about Thursday?"

I screwed up my face. "You expect me to know *that*? Thursday is still two days away!"

"Well, excuse me." Kelly rolled his eyes. "We wouldn't want you thinking ahead now, would we? You might hurt your brain." Then he shoved me and took off.

So, of course, I took off after him. But since I was lugging the garbage bag — and Kelly's faster than me anyway — he was at the school before I was barely halfway across the field. When I finally caught up to him, he was pressed against the wall, peering around the corner.

Without even glancing in my direction, he held up a warning hand. So I dropped the bag and covered the remaining distance on tiptoe.

"What's up?" I whispered, trying to see around him.

He put a finger to his lips. "Listen."

At first, all I could hear was the clipping of shears. Then there was a voice, but it sure wasn't the Mann's.

"What's *she* doing here?" I hissed.

"She's a volunteer — remember?" Kelly whispered back.

"That's during the day," I protested. "She's not supposed to be here after school!"

Kelly shushed me. "Just listen, will ya?"

I could feel myself scowling. For some reason, the idea of Mrs. Butterman talking to the Mann really bugged me. I know it sounds corny, but I think of the Mann as one of the good guys, and Butterman is definitely one of the bad guys, so it was sort of like the Mann was fraternizing with the enemy, and I couldn't help worrying that Mrs. Butterman was going to turn him into a male version of her! I shuddered. Then my curiosity got the better of me, and I strained to hear what they were saying.

"These cedars are gorgeous," Mrs. Butterman gushed. "With all the abuse they take, I'd expect them to be dead, but just look at them — full, green, supple — they're anything *but* dead! Absolutely gorgeous," she said again. "You have to tell me your secret."

"There's no secret, Mrs. Butterman," the Mann replied. "A little water, some fertilizer, an occasional trim with the shears, and some burlap cover in the winter."

Mrs. Butterman laughed. "You're just being modest. There has to be more to it than that, because that's how I care for my cedars and, as you can see, they're not nearly so healthy as these ones."

The shears stopped their clipping, and I didn't need to peek around the corner to know that the Mann was looking across the street toward Mrs. Butterman's house.

"Hmmm," he said after a fairly long pause. "I see what you mean. They do look a bit rough, all right, Mrs. Butterman. If you like, I can come and have a look at them sometime."

"Would you?" she answered in a surprised voice, as if his offer was totally unexpected. "I would really appreciate that. And please ... call me Edna."

The Mann cleared his throat. "It's no problem at all — " pause " — Edna. I have a game to umpire this evening, but if tomorrow is convenient for you, I could stop by after school."

Their conversation was becoming more revolting by the second, and if I listened to another word I was going to be sick. I stomped back to pick up the garbage bag, and the — making as much noise as I could — clomped around the corner of the school.

"Hurry up, Kelly," I hollered over my shoulder. "Let's get out of here."

At the sight of us, the smile on Mrs. Butterman's face melted away.

"It's you two," she said, looking like she'd just swallowed a worm.

I plunked the garbage bag down on the sidewalk in front of the Mann.

"It's good to see you too, Mrs. Butterman," I said as sarcastically as I dared. I didn't need her calling my house again.

Kelly looked her right in the eye and grinned his most annoying grin.

"Yeah, it's us, all right," he sighed. " Firebugs, litterbugs, tomato bugs … " He shrugged. "Just general, all-purpose little bu — "

"I think you boys are done here for the day," the Mann cut him off. "Thank you for your services. Now head on home and get some dinner before your game."

Kelly looked like he was about to say something else, but then he must've changed his mind, because he just shrugged and started jogging toward the street.

So, of course, I was right behind him.

CHAPTER 7

Mom had just started dishing up supper when I walked in the back door. I could tell by the smell that it was my regular pre-game meal — canned spaghetti and chopped-up wieners. My parents were having something else, but spaghetti and wieners is a tradition with me. I just wouldn't feel right heading to the baseball field without my spaghetti. It would be like trying to play without my glove.

As for my dad, Mom could've fed him cardboard that night, and I don't think he would have noticed. He was too busy staring at a bunch of papers scattered around his plate. I'm not allowed to read at the table — not that I would want to — but it's okay for him. *Do as I say, not as I do* — that's what he's always telling me. Basically, what that means is he gets to do all kinds of stuff that I'd get killed for.

My spaghetti was kind of hot, so I tossed it around with my fork a bit and watched the steam rise out of it. Then I looked across the table at my dad. With his eyes glued to the papers, he scooped up a forkful of food, stuffed it in his mouth and chewed — well, sort of, if moving his mouth every three or four seconds can be counted as chewing. Then he frowned at the papers, shuffled them a bit and finally swallowed.

"What're you reading, Dad?" I asked, slurping up a piece of spaghetti. The sauce accidentally sprayed onto one of his papers.

"For crying out loud, Midge!" he grumbled, transferring his frown to me and dabbing at the splotch of spaghetti sauce with his napkin.

"One of the reasons we don't read at the table," Mom told the pork chop she was cutting.

Dad muttered something I didn't catch, but swept the papers onto an empty chair.

"What is all that stuff?" I tried again.

"Umpire exams," he replied, reaching for a slice of bread.

"Umpire exams?" I repeated. "Since when do umpires have to take exams?"

"Since now," he said, slathering butter onto his bread. "It's a new rule. There have been too many inconsistencies in the way the games are being called. Everybody seems to have a different take on the rules. Some umps are calling things that others are letting slide." He screwed up his face and waved his knife at me. "You know how it is. Anyway, there have been complaints. And with the playoffs coming up, the league wants to make sure that everybody is on the same page."

"But the playoffs start this weekend," I reminded him.

"Don't I know it. That's why everybody has to write this exam tomorrow night." Then he glared at my mother. "Which is why I was trying to familiarize myself with the darn thing during supper. It's the only chance I'm going to have."

Mom looked up from her dinner and smiled at him. "Are you talking to me, dear?" she said.

"What happens if somebody fails this test?" I asked.

Dad jerked his thumb over his shoulder. "They're out."

I thought about that for a few mouthfuls. It seemed a little harsh. Sure, there were times when I disagreed with the umps' calls, but all that proved was that they made mistakes. It didn't mean they didn't know the rules. In which case, I told myself, it was unlikely that any of them would fail. But if they *did*, then it probably was better to get rid of them. So maybe this exam wasn't such a bad idea after all.

As Kelly and I had expected, Freddie Bartlett pitched for the Barons that night, but it didn't help — we won anyway. So no matter what happened in the next game, we would finish the season in first place. And that meant Coach Bryant could save Kelly for the playoffs. Somebody else would be pitching against the Lightning.

There was just Mom and me for supper Thursday night, so we both had spaghetti and wieners.

"Where's Dad?" I asked.

"I'm not really sure," she said, "other than he's taking care of some umpire thing. He blew through here like a tornado, grabbed a cold chicken leg and muttered something about schedule changes."

"Schedule changes? Why is he making schedule changes? Did somebody call in sick?"

Mom shrugged. "Not to my knowledge."

I was puzzled. If nobody was sick, why was Dad changing the schedule? Then there was a *ping* inside my brain. I put my fork down and leaned toward my mother. "Did somebody fail that test last night?"

"I wouldn't know," she said a little too quickly.

I couldn't help grinning. My mom is a terrible liar. Her face was already beet red. "I think your nose is growing, Pinnocchio," I teased.

Mom clucked her tongue, then jumped up from the table and hurried over to the counter with her plate. "Now you're just being silly. Hurry up and finish your dinner or you'll be late for your game," she scolded me, as she dumped her supper into the garbage.

So that was it! Somebody *had* failed the exam. But who?

I wolfed down the rest of my food. "See you at the game, Mom!" I yelled, grabbing my glove and slamming out of the house.

"No, I don't have any proof, but I do know my mom, and she was definitely hiding something," I said. "And I'd bet my Alex Rodriguez rookie card I know what it is. One of the umps bombed that test. I'm sure of it. The only thing I don't know is which one. What do you think?"

"Beats me," Kelly said, "but it would have to be somebody who never umps behind the plate. There's no way a person could fake that."

I nodded. If Kelly was right, that really cut down the possibilities. There couldn't be more than two or three guys who only worked the bases.

I had just started thinking about who they were when the coach sent us out to the field for our warm-up. When I booted the very first ball that came at me, I decided maybe I should concentrate on the game instead of the umpires. And anyway, the mystery wasn't that hard to solve. All I had to do was ask my dad.

Back in the dugout, Coach Bryant went over the roster. He said he wanted the whole team sharp for the playoffs, so we were all going to get into the game that night. Half the usual starters would begin along with half the bench, and then at the end of the fourth inning, he would change everybody up. I was on the second shift.

Just before the game got underway, I saw my dad arrive and squeeze onto the bleachers behind home plate. Since I wasn't scheduled to play until later, I thought about wandering over and solving the mystery right then.

But the loudspeaker guy started announcing the teams, and I got to thinking it might not be such a good idea after all. Whoever the ump was, he was probably feeling stupid enough without having everyone at the ballpark know he'd failed the test.

Then the players took the field and the umpire yelled, "Play ball."

"Hey, Midge." Barry Martin nudged me and pointed toward home plate. "I thought the Mann was supposed to be calling tonight's game."

Because I was sort of preoccupied, it took a few seconds for Barry's words to penetrate my brain, and then when they did, I wished they hadn't.

The mystery was solved.

CHAPTER 8

It was a good thing I wasn't playing the first few innings, because I don't think I would have been able to make my body move onto the field. I was having enough trouble just getting my brain to work. I was totally stunned. It was like finding out the truth about Santa Claus all over again.

How could the Mann have possibly failed the umpire test? There was more chance of my family moving to Jupiter than there was of him blowing that test. He was just too smart. He knew too much about baseball. He could've been the one who made that test up, for Pete's sake. No. There had to be some other explanation.

Even with our bench in and without Kelly pitching, we won the game, though it took us to the bottom of the ninth to do it. As soon as it was over, I hopped on my bike and pedaled home so fast you would've thought I was in the Olympics. I had to talk to my dad. I had to find out the truth — one way or the other.

But I guess I was a little too fast, because I even beat my parents home. I paced back and forth in front of the living room window, waiting for their car to pull into the driveway. After twenty minutes I went outside and peered down the street. But there was still no sign of them.

When they finally did arrive, they were carrying a couple of grocery bags. They'd obviously stopped at the market on the way home.

"Dad," I blurted the second they came through the door, "did the Mann fail that test?"

My parents stopped dead in their tracks and looked at each other in a way that sent my hopes crashing to the floor.

Then Dad passed the bag he was carrying to my mom, and she continued on to the kitchen. We both watched her, and when she finally disappeared down the hall, Dad turned back to me. He cleared his throat, and his eyebrows kind of joined up over his nose to give him that stern look he gets whenever he's going to punish me for something. To my amazement, he shook his head.

"No," he said. "He didn't."

I was so relieved, my knees went weak, and I sank onto the couch.

"*Phew*!" I said, wiping pretend sweat from my forehead. "I knew he couldn't have bombed it.

I knew it. He's way too smart. But when Mom said you had to make schedule changes, and then the Mann didn't show up at the game, I started to think the worst. Pretty dopey, eh?" I rolled my eyes and grinned. Then I had another thought and stopped smiling. "So why *wasn't* he umping my game tonight? "

"Because he never wrote the test," Dad said.

Whoa! I hadn't seen that one coming, and it took me a couple of seconds to make sense of what my dad had said. Then I remembered the Mann and Mrs. Butterman making plans to look at her cedars. But that was crazy! There was no way the Mann would've passed up his umpire exam for *that*. Just the same, I had to be sure.

"Maybe he was doing something else Wednesday night," I suggested cautiously.

Dad shook his head again. "No. No, it wasn't that. He showed up at the community center along with everybody else."

Now I was really puzzled.

"So why didn't he write the test?"

That's when my dad exploded.

"Because he's a proud, pig-headed fool!" he shouted.

I stared at my dad in disbelief.

"I thought you liked the Mann," I protested. "You said he was the best umpire you'd ever seen outside the majors."

"He is!" Dad was still yelling.

Mom's head appeared in the doorway. "Gary,

you're shouting," she told him as the rest of her followed her head into the room.

"I am not shouting!" he shouted, and then more quietly, as if he was trying to convince himself, "I am not shouting."

There was a pause as we all waited for Dad's blood pressure to go down. Finally he took a deep breath and told me what had happened.

"He *refused* to write the test?" I repeated in disbelief. "But why?"

"Because he's a — "

"Gary." Mom raised a warning eyebrow.

Dad held up his hand like a traffic cop. "It's okay, Doris. I'm not going to yell." Then he turned back to me. "Hal said that having to write a test was an insult. He said that he has been officiating baseball for twenty years, and if the league didn't know by now whether or not he could do the job, then they'd better find someone else to do it. If he hadn't proven himself yet, he certainly wouldn't be able to do it on a piece of paper."

That made sense to me.

"Anyway," Dad continued, "I tried to explain that the test was just a formality. It had nothing to do with him personally. *His* credentials weren't in question, but the league couldn't very well make some umpires take a test and not others."

"What did he say to that?"

"He said it didn't make any difference. It was the principle of the thing. He said it used to be that community baseball welcomed all the volunteers it could get, whether they knew much about the game or not, because the important thing was providing kids with an opportunity to play. But now that umpires get a token payment, the league thinks it has the right to make all kinds of demands. Hal said he wasn't looking for a pat on the back, but this test made him feel like all his years of umping didn't count for anything."

At the risk of sending my dad off the deep end again, I said, "It does kind of seem that way."

"You're right, Midge. It does," Mom agreed.

Dad sank down on the couch beside me and sighed. "I know it does. But aside from assuring him that we do appreciate his efforts, there's not a thing I can do."

"Can't you at least try to make the league see things Hal's way?" Mom asked.

"Yeah. Can't you?" I chimed in.

Dad shook his head. "There's no point. The bigwigs have made up their minds. And when it comes right down to it, I agree with them — in principle, anyway. Implementing standards is a good thing. And the test does that. The only problem is it doesn't take into consideration people like Hal Mann."

Mom clucked her tongue and frowned. "Well, if you ask me, I think it would be a real shame if the league loses a fine umpire over something as trivial as this test. I guess we'll just have to hope he changes his mind and agrees to write it."

"But what if he doesn't?" I asked. "What will you do then, Dad?"

He spread his hands in defeat. "There's nothing I can do. My hands are tied. I have to follow the rules. Unless Hal agrees to take the test, I can't allow him to umpire any more games."

"Even though he's the best umpire in the whole league?" I couldn't believe what my dad was saying.

"Yes."

This time it was me who yelled. "Well, that's just plain dumb!"

Mom's eyebrow shot up again.

"Maybe so," Dad conceded, "but it's still the rule."

"Well, it's a stupid rule, and somebody should do something to change it!" I fumed.

Dad shrugged. "Maybe somebody will."

CHAPTER 9

... maybe somebody will ... maybe somebody will ... maybe somebody will ...

For the rest of the evening, I couldn't get those words out of my head. It was like they'd been Krazy Glued to my brain, getting in the way of everything else I was thinking. It reminded me of when I was a little kid, and Mom would send me to the store. All the way there, a tiny voice would keep repeating the thing I was supposed to get. The rest of my brain would be doing other stuff, like looking for puddles to ride my bike through or wondering what was for supper, but that little tape recorder would keep playing in the background — *a loaf of bread ... a loaf of bread ... a loaf of bread.* The thing is, even after I got what I'd been sent for, the voice would keep on talking, and it could take hours before it finally got tired and shut up.

Maybe somebody will …

I fell into bed, pounded my pillow into a ball and pulled the covers up to my chin. Then I took a deep breath and waited for my body to melt and for my mind to slide into thinking about baseball — that's how I go to sleep. But something was wrong. Things weren't working like they were supposed to. *Maybe somebody will* was getting in the way. And it was really starting to bug me.

Why couldn't I get those stupid words out of my head?

There had to be a reason. Was it possible that *maybe somebody will* was a subconscious suggestion my dad had used to try to tell me something? Yeah, right — as if my dad was that tricky. Anyway, what could he have been trying to say? That I was the one who should do something about the league's new rule?

I rolled over.

What could *I* do? If my dad couldn't change things — and he was president of the umpires' association — there was no way the league was going to pay attention to me.

I kicked the blankets loose, flipped onto my back and stared at the ceiling.

But if *somebody* didn't do something, we were going to lose the Mann.

On the way to school the next morning, I told Kelly

about the Mann and the test. Kelly didn't say a word — just picked up a rock and pegged off a flower hanging over the sidewalk. *Thwack!* Red petals fluttered to the pavement, and the rock ricocheted off a car in the street.

We kept walking. Kelly threw a few more rocks and kicked a couple of others. When we got to the edge of the schoolyard, he leaned against a *No Parking* sign. Then he squinted up at the sun.

"You know," he said, "I was just thinking."

"Oh, yeah," I said.

He nodded. "Yeah. I was thinking about what Miss Drummond said the other day in English class. You know, when she was telling us that stuff about language being a living thing because of how it's always changing? How new words get invented and old ones die out?"

"Yeah," I said. I sort of remembered the lesson he was talking about, though I was kind of surprised that he did.

He nodded some more. "Yeah. I've been thinking about that."

Now he had me curious, and I waited for him to get to the point. But he didn't.

"*And*?" I said, hoping that would get him moving again.

It did.

"And I've thought of a word we should get rid of."

"What's that?" I asked.

But he didn't answer me. Wherever Kelly was

going with this conversation, he was going at his own speed. There was no point rushing him. So, we both just stood there, looking up at the sun and saying nothing. Eventually he started talking again.

"Miss Drummond said that when a word loses its meaning, it becomes … what did she call it?" His forehead knotted as he hunted for the right term. "It starts with an 'O'. Ob – ob – ob something."

"Obsolete?" I suggested.

Kelly's face cleared. "Right. That's what she said. It becomes obsolete." Then his expression got serious again. "Well, I know a word that is obsolete."

"What's that?" I asked for the second time.

"Fair," he said, pushing himself away from the *No Parking* sign and heading for the school.

"Fair?" I echoed. "How do you figure that's obsolete?"

"Think about it," he said. "What does it mean?"

"Well, it's … " I started and then stopped. It was hard to explain. It's weird how that is, how you can know something perfectly well, but not be able to put it into words. I tried again. "It means that everybody gets treated the same. And it means that you get what you deserve."

Kelly shot me an *I-told-you-so* glance.

"There you go," he said.

But I still didn't understand what he was getting at, and I told him so.

Kelly looked as if he was trying to decide if I was pulling his leg. Finally, in a totally matter-of-fact voice, he said, "Fairness doesn't exist, so why should there be a word for it?"

I wasn't used to this philosophical side of Kelly, and anyway, whatever he was getting at required more thinking than I was willing to do at 8:45 in the morning.

So I said, "Why do you say fairness doesn't exist?"

"Because it doesn't. If it did, the world would be a lot different."

"In what way?"

He shrugged. "In lots of ways."

"Like what?"

Kelly had been taking so long to say whatever it was he was trying to say that I was getting kind of drowsy, but when the next words exploded out of his mouth, I totally woke up again.

"Like, for one thing, everybody would start out equal. People wouldn't be mean to other people just because they're poor or because they don't speak English very well, or because they don't have big important jobs. Nobody would get judged because of their clothes or where they live — stuff like that. Everybody would have a chance to prove themselves."

We'd reached the front of the school. Through the window we could see the Mann cleaning the glass of the trophy case. Kelly watched him for a minute and then turned back to me.

"And if there was such a thing as fair," he said, "the Mann wouldn't have to write that test."

By noon, Kelly's philosophical mood had passed, and he was back to kidding around with everybody and grinning like an orthodontic poster child.

We dumped our books into our lockers and headed for the lunchroom. Some of the guys were already there, and I started to make my way over to them, but Kelly grabbed my arm and dragged me to an empty table on the other side of the room.

"What's up?" I said.

"I've got an idea," he told me, sliding onto the bench.

I recognized the gleam in his eye.

"You've always got an idea," I said. "That's why Mrs. MacDonald has a filing cabinet in her office just for us."

"Nah, it's nothing like that," he snickered. "I've got an idea how we can get the Mann umping again without him writing that test."

I eyed Kelly suspiciously.

"Does it involve hiring hit men to rub out the league officials who made up the test?" I asked. "Because I'm pretty sure I'd get grounded for that."

"Ha, ha. You are such a funny guy," Kelly said. "Do you want to hear my idea or not?"

I took a bite of my sandwich. "Since when do I have a choice? And anyway, if it gets the Mann back umping, I'm in."

Kelly leaned across the table and lowered his voice. "Okay then. Here's what we're going to do."

CHAPTER 10

The weather was perfect for the first day of the playoffs. It had rained during the night — just enough to kill the dust on the field — but by morning the clouds were already clearing off, and it wasn't long before the sky was completely blue.

Nervousness was fizzing in my stomach like someone had exploded a bottle of pop in there, and since I couldn't sit still I headed to the ballpark early. The diamond was ready to go. It had been freshly lined and mowed in a criss-cross pattern so that it looked like green plaid. The pitcher's mound had been raked, and there were even new bags on the bases. I sat in the dugout, breathing everything in and pounding the pocket of my glove to calm my jitters.

Ours was the first game on the schedule — us against the Carey Hill Panthers. The Panthers hadn't given us much competition during the regular season, but you still couldn't write them off. Anything could happen in the playoffs.

The fans started arriving even before the teams showed up, and by game time the park was packed. Of course, my dad was in his usual spot. I'm not sure how he manages to snag that seat behind home plate every single game, but he does. At first I didn't see my mom, but that's because she wasn't in the bleachers. She'd brought lawn chairs and set them up along the third-base line for her and Ms. Romani.

It seemed like the whole town had come out for the game, with maybe two exceptions — Mrs. Butterman and the Mann. I've never seen Mrs. Butterman at a game, so it would have been more of a surprise if she *had* shown up, but I'd sort of thought the Mann would be there.

The pre-game ceremonies took forever. First there was the official welcoming of the teams and fans by the league president. Then there was a history lesson on baseball in our district, followed by an explanation of how the playoff ladder worked. Eventually there was the introduction of the teams. By that time I was so tense, my knees were bouncing. But when my name was announced over the loudspeaker, I managed to run out to the field and line up along the third-base side with the rest of my team.

I gazed down the line at the other guys. Most of them looked like they were about to face a firing squad. I squinted across the field at the Panthers.

They didn't look any better.

Finally the officials came out — three of them for the playoffs instead of the usual two — and it was time to start the game.

"Let's play ball!" the home plate umpire shouted, and the excited crowd roared its approval.

I took a deep breath. This was it.

But instead of taking our positions on the field like we were supposed to, we all stayed right where we were. None of the Rebels moved a muscle. The Panthers held their ground too.

"Play ball," the umpire called again.

He might as well have been talking to the backstop.

A curious buzz spread through the bleachers as the fans began to realize something was wrong. "Ricky, get out there!" somebody's mother yelled. I was glad it wasn't mine. It was bad enough feeling Mom's eyes boring into my back. I didn't need her hollering at me too. The officials on the field looked at one another and then at my dad.

Then both coaches came flying out of the dugouts.

"Have you kids completely lost your minds? What the heck are you trying to prove?" Coach Bryant exploded.

He marched down the line, scowling at each of us, but no one even flinched — at least, not when he was looking.

So he tried another approach.

"Talk to me!" he said in a voice so quiet and

calm, it was scarier than his yelling had been.

There was still no response. We could've been statues.

The coach clenched his fists — and his teeth. He began jabbing at the air as if he was an out-of-control marionette. "This is no time to play games," he growled. "We have a game to play here!" Then, realizing he'd completely contradicted himself, he snatched his ball cap off his head and drop kicked it into the dirt. "You kids are going to be the death of me!" He was back to yelling. "When I get to the bottom of this, I'm going to …"

Suddenly his eyes narrowed, and he stomped down the line of players until he got to Kelly. Then he stuck his big head into Kelly's face until their noses were practically touching.

"Romani," he seethed, "this stunt has your name written all over it. All I can say is, you better have a darn good reason for it, because if you don't — playoffs or no playoffs — you can consider yourself benched! And that's a promise."

My gaze drifted to the other side of the diamond. The Panthers had broken ranks and were now huddled around their coach.

I nudged Jerry Fletcher. But before he could pass the message along, the Panthers' coach pushed his way out of the tangle of players and started jogging across the field.

"Dag," he called. And then louder, "Dag!"

Coach Bryant gave Kelly one last glare before

joining the other coach on the mound. Then the two of them put their heads together and began talking, but they were so quiet I couldn't make out a single word.

My dad had joined the umpires at home plate, and the four of them were holding their own meeting, glancing toward the two coaches every now and then to see how things were progressing there. Finally — strung out in a line like the Earp brothers at the OK Corral — the umpires headed to the mound.

The fans were becoming restless.

"What's the holdup?" somebody yelled. "Are you gonna play or aren't ya?"

A few people left their seats and made their way to the Panther dugout, looking for an explanation. There might have been people at our dugout too — I didn't know. My team was still standing in a line facing first base.

We wanted everyone to realize that we weren't kidding around. This wasn't just a prank to get attention. We were dead serious. Until the league reconsidered its position and let the Mann ump again, we weren't going to play.

There wasn't a kid in the league who didn't feel the same way about the Mann as we did, so it hadn't been hard to get the Panthers to go along with the protest too. It didn't matter that they'd weakened and told their coach what was going on. Somebody would have had to spill the beans sooner or later.

After much head scratching and arm waving, the little group at the mound finally reached a decision. At any rate, both coaches headed back to their teams.

Coach Bryant planted himself in front of us and squinted up and down the line a couple of times. Then he shook his head and ran his hand through his thinning hair. He looked a bit shell-shocked, but at least he wasn't mad anymore.

"You kids are something else," he said. There was more than a little amazement in his voice. He paused and looked at us some more. "Yeah — something else. And I want you to know that, in a way, I admire you for doing what you're doing. Believe me, I want the Mann out here umping just as much as you do. I think everybody does. And you kids could be right. He might be getting a raw deal." Coach Bryant shrugged. "That's not for me to say."

He paused again and looked at us some more.

"The thing is — this ... this protest thing you're doing, it's not going to accomplish anything — well, at least not what you want it to. The only thing that's going to happen is that you're going to get knocked out of the playoffs."

We all exchanged startled glances.

"What do you mean?" Pete Jacobs broke the team silence.

Coach Bryant looked over his shoulder at the umpires on the mound. Then he turned back to us.

"I mean that if you boys don't get onto the field and start playing ball within the next five minutes, you're going to default the game."

We exchanged looks again.

"How can we default if the Panthers won't play either?" someone asked.

"The Panthers will default too. The umpires will hand both teams a loss."

"Can they do that?" Barry asked.

Coach Bryant nodded. "They can, and they will. So think very carefully about what you want to do here. Two losses and you're out of the playoffs." Then he took a step back and extended his hands, palms up. "It's your decision. You have two minutes to talk it over."

CHAPTER 11

It was only one loss.

That's what we told ourselves as we left the park. One loss. We weren't out of the playoffs yet. Besides, the Panthers were in the same boat as we were. So were the Barons and the Whips. Their game was right after ours, and they'd defaulted too.

There were only two teams who hadn't had a game yet — the Lightning and the Demons. They were supposed to play on Sunday, and if they protested too, the league would really start to feel the pressure.

Unfortunately, my dad already was. The phone was ringing when we got home from the ballpark, and it kept right on ringing the entire afternoon. Parents, fans, umpires, even the lady who runs the concession — they all wanted to know what was going on.

My dad answered their questions — at least, as well as he could. It made me feel kind of bad. I hadn't realized our protest was going to put him on the spot like that. When I think about it, though, I guess I should have. But the plan had seemed so simple. *We protest — the Mann gets to ump.* I hadn't thought about all the stuff that was going to happen in between.

At suppertime, Mom turned off the ringer on the phone.

"Enough is enough. You can at least have your dinner in peace and quiet," she told Dad.

The meal was quiet, all right — you could hear every chomp and slurp and swallow. Judging from the grooves in Dad's forehead, though, it wasn't all that peaceful. He was obviously thinking about what had happened at the ballpark. But he didn't seem angry, and that sort of puzzled me, because — for once — I wouldn't have blamed him for being mad. In fact, I was ready for it.

And that was something new for me. You see, even though I get in trouble a lot, I don't usually see it coming. Sometimes I don't even know I've messed up until I'm getting heck for it. This time it was different, though. This time I knew what we were doing was going to upset people, but I was prepared for the consequences. The thing is there didn't seem to be any.

Halfway through supper, Dad looked across at me and said, "Is this it then? Or will there be more?"

I thought about the game coming up on Sunday and cringed. "There's probably gonna be more," I confessed.

He didn't seem surprised. In fact, he didn't seem anything at all. He just nodded and turned back to his supper.

"Sorry," I mumbled guiltily.

Dad didn't even look up. "You gotta do what you gotta do," he said.

I spent the evening thinking about that — *that* and a lot of other stuff.

Like the fact that if my team protested another game — and there was a real chance we might have to — our baseball season was over. We would go from championship favorites to major losers — without ever picking up a bat! I sure hoped it wouldn't turn out that way, but if it did, I knew I'd see it through. I had to. My dad was right about that.

If somebody had asked me a week earlier, I would have said nothing could be more important than baseball — especially the championship. But suddenly things had changed. This business with the Mann *was* more important. Not just because he was a great guy and a super umpire — which he was — and not even because all the players would miss him — which we would. If it had been the Mann's idea to quit umping, we still would have thought he was the best and we'd still have missed him, but we would have accepted his decision.

The thing is, it *wasn't* his decision. He was being pushed out, and all because the league was letting a stupid rule be more important than a person. Even I could see how wrong that was. But the grown-ups weren't doing anything to fix the situation, so it was up to us kids. Talk about a mixed-up world! Here I was, fighting for a principle, and until a couple of days ago, I hadn't even known I had any!

The Demons-Lightning game on Sunday got rained out, which — according to my dad — was a blessing in disguise, because if it had been boycotted, the season could have ended right then. As it was, the league was holding an emergency meeting that night, and it might cancel the rest of the games anyway.

Or, I pointed out to my dad, it might reconsider its rule on making umpires write a test. Dad admitted that was a possibility too. Whatever was going to happen, it was going to be decided at that meeting.

Naturally I was all set to go, until my dad told me it wasn't open to the public. *He* wasn't even allowed to attend, although — being the head umpire — it was a pretty safe bet he'd be one of the first people to find out the results.

The meeting started at seven o'clock. By eight, I was staring at the phone. By nine, I was pacing with it. By nine-thirty, it still hadn't rung, and I was beginning to give up hope, so when it suddenly jangled in my hand, I was so startled I practically threw it on the floor.

"Hello," I said, juggling the receiver to my ear. There was no answer. Then the phone rang a second time.

"You might want to turn it on," said my dad, who'd suddenly appeared out of nowhere.

I felt like an idiot. "I knew that," I muttered as I punched the button. "Hello," I said again.

This time there was a man's voice at the other end. "May I speak to Gary Ridge, please?"

My stomach did a flip. This was it. This was the call from the league. The meeting was finally over.

"Just a minute," I mumbled, passing my dad the phone.

"Hello," he said into the receiver. And then, "Ah, Bill. So — how did it go?"

I held my breath while I waited for the answer. But fifteen minutes later, I was still waiting. All my dad had said the whole time was, *Uh-huh, yes, I see, go on, oh boy,* and *really,* which didn't tell me a whole lot.

So he'd barely hung up the phone before I was bombarding him with questions.

"*Whoa.*" He put up both hands. "Slow down. I can't answer fifteen questions at one time. If you want to know what happened, sit down and I'll tell you — *my way.*"

Reluctantly, I slid onto a kitchen chair. Knowing my dad, this could take forever. He poured himself a coffee and sat down too.

"Well, it seems the board was split," he began. "At least, it was at the start of the meeting. Three of the members wanted to cancel the remaining games, and the other three wanted to give you boys a chance to change your minds ..." he paused " ... or default yourselves out of the playoffs."

My mouth fell open. "You mean they never even *considered* taking back that stupid test rule?" I protested.

Dad frowned at me. "I thought we agreed that I was going to get to tell this my way."

"Fine," I grumbled, and sat back in my chair.

"Anyway," Dad continued, "they wanted to hear what Hal had to say before they made their — "

"The Mann was there?" I lurched forward in my chair once more.

"Are you going to let me tell this or aren't you?" Dad frowned.

"Yeah, but — " I started to argue.

He pushed his chair back from the table.

"Okay," I conceded quickly. A snail could've told the story faster. Just the same, I didn't want my dad not to tell it at all. "Okay. I won't say another word," I promised, and then when it looked like he was going to carry on, I added, "But could you go a little faster? The suspense is killing me."

He picked up right where I'd interrupted him

— at exactly the same speed. "They wanted to talk to Hal before they made their final decision. They wanted to make sure he hadn't put you boys up to this boycott."

I literally had to bite my tongue to keep from protesting again. The Mann would *never* have asked us to do that! It was obvious the board didn't know Hal Mann at all.

"Of course, Hal assured them that he hadn't known anything about it. Then the board members asked him if he would reconsider writing the test. He said he wouldn't. Then he asked them if they would reconsider making the test mandatory. They said they couldn't."

"So what's gonna happen now?" I asked, and then, remembering I wasn't supposed to be talking, I clapped my hand over my mouth.

Dad didn't seem to notice.

"The board decided to base its ruling on the next game. If the Demons and Lightning both refuse to play, then all six playoff teams will have made a stand. And since the board isn't going to change its decision about the test, there would be no point in scheduling any more games for you kids *not* to play. And that would be that. The season would be over."

He folded his arms on the table and looked across at me. "So it looks like it's up to you boys."

CHAPTER 12

On the way to school the next morning I told Kelly what had happened at the meeting.

"They're bluffing," he said.

But I wasn't so sure. It had sounded like they were pretty serious to me.

"What if they're not?" I knew the answer to that question as well as Kelly did, but I was hoping he might have a Plan B hiding up his sleeve somewhere.

He yanked open the door of the school and headed inside. "I guess we'll find out at the next game," he said.

That's exactly what I was afraid of.

With five minutes until the morning bell, the school halls were wall-to-wall kids — elbowing their way to lockers, gabbing and laughing, dropping books, fighting with locks, slamming doors, and just generally revving up for the day.

I already had everything for the morning's

classes, so I leaned against my locker and waited for Kelly. He dialed in his combo and tugged open the lock. Then he banged on the top of the door with his fist. He has one of those lockers that stick, and banging on the door is the only way to get it open — though I'm not really sure why anyone would want to.

I'm not a neat freak or anything, but I have to say that Kelly has the messiest locker I've ever seen. There could be a body in there and nobody would ever find it. The entire inside is one massive tangle of papers, books, gym clothes, candy wrappers, juice boxes, shoes, jackets — and a billion other things! You'd think the stuff would fall out when Kelly opens the door, but it doesn't. That's because it can't! Everything is crammed in so tight, it's like one of those junkyard cars that's been crunched into a cube.

Kelly glanced at the timetable taped to the inside of the door. Then he stuck his hand into the middle of the mess and hauled out a black binder and two textbooks. Right away all the other stuff shifted down to fill the gaps, and the inside of Kelly's locker became a solid block of junk again.

I made a face. "Are you ever gonna clean that thing?"

Kelly seemed surprised. "What for? I know where everything is."

Behind him, I saw the Mann coming down the hall with some fluorescent lighting tubes in his arms. He walked past without even slowing down or looking at us, but the way Kelly's head suddenly swung around, I knew the Mann must've said something.

Kelly closed up his locker and headed down the hall after him, gesturing for me to come too.

The Mann led us to his office. Actually, it's the furnace room, but it has a desk and a chair, so I guess that's why he calls it an office. Students aren't supposed to go in there, but since we were with an adult, I didn't think we could get into too much trouble.

The Mann closed the door and sat on the edge of the desk. He didn't waste any time getting to the point.

"This strike has got to stop," he said, and I could tell he meant business. He wasn't asking us to stop protesting; he was telling us to. He sounded just like he does at the ballpark. And that was weird, because the Mann was being his umpire self when he should have been being his custodian self. He'd gotten his personalities mixed up. The tired gray uniform and the furnace room both said *janitor*, but the attitude was definitely *umpire*.

"I know you boys are the ones behind this." He rested his hands on the desktop and leaned back, like he was waiting for us to argue with him. "You are the ones who rallied the troops, and now it's time to *un*rally them." Then he looked at me. "I'm sure your dad has told you what's going to happen if you don't."

Kelly let out a groan.

"Aw, c'mon. Get serious! They're not going to cancel the playoffs!" He stomped across the room in three steps and then spun around. "They're just bluffing! Can't you see that? They're trying to scare us."

"Well, I hope they've succeeded," the Mann shot back.

Kelly dug in his heels and frowned. "We're not quitting."

The Mann shook his head. "Now you're just being stubborn."

"And you're not?" Kelly retorted. "This whole thing started because you wouldn't write that test. All the players are doing is trying to help you out."

The Mann heaved a giant sigh, and his chin dropped onto his chest. Eventually he looked up again.

"I know that," he said. "And don't think that I don't appreciate the gesture. I do — very much." He paused. "It was a good idea, but it's not going to work. The board has made its decision, and carrying on with this protest isn't going to change it."

"You don't know that," Kelly argued. "When it gets down to the crunch, the board will give in."

"It's unlikely."

"No, it isn't. Adults are always making threats they don't follow through on. I'm telling you, this is nothing but a scare tactic," Kelly insisted.

The Mann looked at him hard. "And what if it isn't? What if you're wrong? You're always so darn sure of yourself, Kelly, but you could be wrong."

Kelly opened his mouth to protest, but the

Mann cut him off.

"For once in your life, listen! *You could be wrong*! And if you are, the season ends tonight. The second the Demons and the Lightning refuse to take the field, baseball is over for the year. No district championship, no city title, and certainly no shot at provincials."

Kelly stuck out his chin and crossed his arms over his chest.

"I'm willing to take that chance."

To my amazement, the Mann laughed.

"Of course you are. I'd have been surprised if you'd said anything different. You've committed yourself and your pride won't let you back down. Well, I suppose that's your choice. If you want to shoot yourself in the foot, go ahead. But what about the other hundred guys you've dragged into this war? Did it ever occur to you that those boys might not see things the same way you do? Did you even consider the possibility that they might want to make their own decision? Or are you the only one who has that right?"

An uncomfortable silence took over the room. It felt like it went on forever, but eventually it was broken — by the bell. Wonderful! Now, on top of everything else, we were late!

The Mann stood up and opened the door.

"C'mon," he said. "You boys have to get to class. I'll tell the office that you were helping me with something, and they'll give you a late pass."

Without a word, Kelly stalked out of the room. I started to follow him, but the Mann stopped me at the door.

He put his hand on my shoulder, and there was almost a pleading look in his eyes as he said, "You're Kelly's friend, Midge. Maybe you can get him to see reason."

CHAPTER 13

It wasn't going to be easy getting Kelly "to see reason," as the Mann put it, especially since I was having trouble seeing it myself. The situation had become pretty complicated. It sort of reminded me of Kelly's locker.

There was a part of me that agreed with the Mann — at least about the guys deserving a chance to choose for themselves. But I could see Kelly's side of it too. After all, what was the point of having principles if you didn't stick to them? And what kind of friend would I be if I left Kelly to fight this thing alone? As far as I was concerned, if the protests weren't going to get us what we wanted, there didn't seem much use in going on with them. I'd rather play baseball. But if Kelly wasn't going to give in, then I couldn't either.

My only hope was to try to get him to change

his mind. Not that I thought talking would do that, but I had to at least try — and I had to do it in a hurry!

I decided to take a shot in Science. We were doing a lab that morning, and since labs are generally pretty noisy, it seemed like the perfect opportunity. The problem was how to bring the subject up without setting Kelly off again. But I didn't have to worry about it. Kelly brought it up himself.

"The season isn't going to get canceled," he grumbled when I came back to our station with the lab equipment.

I didn't say anything, partly because it seemed like Kelly was talking to himself, but mostly because there really wasn't anything to say. We'd already been over that topic a bunch of times without solving anything. There didn't seem much point getting into it again. So I just kept on setting up the microscope.

And Kelly kept on thinking out loud.

"Why can't the Mann believe me? He's the one who's being stubborn about everything. It isn't me. If he cares so much about what's happened, he should just write that test. The only reason he's on our case now is because he has a guilty conscience."

I stopped adjusting the focus and said, "About what?"

"About causing this whole mess!"

"But he didn't cause it," I pointed out. "Not really. Okay, so he balked over writing that test, but he had every right to do that. He didn't know the players were going to boycott the playoffs because of it. That was our idea — remember? You might be right about him feeling guilty, but I don't think it's because he didn't write the test. I think it's because the playoffs might get canceled. He doesn't want us guys to miss the rest of the baseball season on account of sticking up for him."

"How many times do I have to tell you? The playoffs aren't going to get canceled," Kelly growled.

"For the rest of your life, if you want," I growled right back. I had no idea how Kelly could be so sure the league would back down, but I was tired of hearing it. "Why don't you give it a rest? Unless we go through with tonight's protest, we're never gonna know."

Kelly stared at me as if I'd just suggested we murder somebody.

"What d'ya mean — *unless*? Don't tell me you want to chicken out!"

"Of course I don't," I defended myself quickly. "That's not what I'm saying."

"Well, what *are* you saying?" He glared at me suspiciously.

I knew I was walking on eggshells. If this next bit didn't come out of my mouth just right, I could end up with a black eye and no best friend.

I took a breath and began. "We started these protests to show the league that it wasn't being fair about the test. Well, it hasn't apologized, and it hasn't taken the test back, so none of that has changed."

Kelly's body relaxed a little. "Good," he almost smiled. "You had me worried there for a minute."

"No fear." I tried to smile back. "If you're sure the league is bluffing, and you're willing to risk the rest of the season on it, then I'm with you."

This time Kelly's grin was real.

"*But* — " I said with emphasis, and the grin disappeared, "I think we've gotta let the other guys make that decision for themselves."

The glare was back, but I had already committed myself. I couldn't back down now. So I played my ace.

"Otherwise, it wouldn't be fair."

I know I didn't talk Kelly into calling off the boycott. Kelly doesn't do anything he doesn't want to do. All I did was offer him a way around his pride.

Just the same, when we met with the Demons and the Lightning before the game, Kelly didn't try to influence them. He didn't give the slightest hint what he wanted them to do. He didn't even say what *he* was going to do. All Kelly did was tell them that the Mann wanted them to play and that the league said the rest of the season would be canceled if they didn't. Then he left them to make their own decision.

And when they had, we got on our bikes and took off.

We rode without talking. Kelly led the way, and I followed behind. I wasn't really paying much attention to where we were going. It didn't matter anyway. I was too busy thinking about what had just happened at the ballpark to care about sight-seeing.

We must have gone on that way — riding and not talking — for a good fifteen minutes or so, but finally Kelly pulled up, so I pulled up behind him. I looked around, wondering why we'd stopped. That's when I realized I had no idea where we were, except that we weren't in our own neighborhood anymore.

We were on a street lined with houses, but there was nothing special about any of them as far as I could tell. They were just little square boxes in little square yards. Some looked more run down than others, but they were all pretty old and dilapidated.

Except for the one Kelly had stopped in front of. It was just as old as the others, but you could tell it was a lot better cared for. The house and the little picket fence surrounding it were both painted a cheery yellow. The grass was free of weeds and neatly cut — even along the edges by the fence — and there were flowers bordering the sidewalk and in planters on the front porch.

Kelly got off his bike and wheeled it into the yard.

"What the heck are you doin'?" I hissed at him. All we needed was to get busted for trespassing.

"It's all right," he called back to me. "C'mon. The Mann is gonna want to know what happened."

CHAPTER 14

There were two things running through my head.

The first one was surprise. I mean, it was one thing to visit the Mann in the school's furnace room, but this was where he lived. This was his house!

I looked it over again. It was exactly the sort of house I would have expected the Mann to have — if I'd expected him to have a house, that is. But that's the thing. *I hadn't*. It's not that I thought he lived in an igloo or a tent or anything. The truth is, I'd never thought about where he lived — period. For all I knew, he could've lived at the school!

Come to think of it, that wasn't such a bad idea. There was a bed in the nurse's room for him to sleep on. He could shower in the guys' change room and cook his food in the teachers' lounge. There was even a washer and dryer in the home economics room for his laundry. It was the perfect set-up.

The second thing running through my head was curiosity. Kelly had zeroed in on the Mann's house like he was a homing pigeon. What I couldn't figure out was how he'd known where the Mann lived. I suppose he could have gotten the address from some list at school, or he could've looked it up in the phone book, but somehow I didn't think so. The way he'd wheeled his bike into the yard, locked it to a pipe on the side of the house and then jogged around to the back said he knew this place. I would've bet my dad's autographed Nolan Ryan baseball on it.

Even so, when he yanked open the screen door and yelled, "Hal, it's me and Midge," I just about fell off the steps.

What the heck was Kelly doing? Even if he *had* been to the Mann's house before — though I couldn't imagine how or why he would've — that still didn't give him the right to barge in without knocking. And what was he thinking, calling the Mann by his first name?

All the hassle about the playoffs had sent Kelly over the edge. That was the only explanation.

In the split second it took me to think all that, Kelly was practically through the door. I made a grab for his shirt, to pull him back.

"Are you nuts?" I squeaked. "Get outta there! You're going to get us expelled for sure, probably thrown in jail too!"

"It's okay," he said, and headed back inside.

Then the Mann's voice drifted through the open door — and he wasn't yelling or anything. "C'mon in, boys," he said.

It looked like Kelly was right. It *was* okay.

I gave my head a good shake. The situation was getting stranger by the minute. I didn't understand any of it, but I wasn't getting any smarter standing in the Mann's backyard thinking about it, so I tromped up the steps and followed Kelly into the house.

The back door opened into a tiny, old-fashioned kitchen. It was nothing fancy — just a few cupboards, a fridge, stove, and a small table with two chairs. In five steps we were through it and into the living room.

That's where the Mann was. He was sitting in one of those fake-leather recliner chairs, watching a baseball game on television.

"Have a seat, boys." Without even taking his eyes off the game, he waved us toward the couch.

So we sat down and proceeded to listen to the game. I say *listen* because there was no way we could watch it. The couch and the television were on the same wall, and even sitting forward and twisting my head backwards, I could barely see the screen. After about twenty seconds my eyeballs started to hurt.

I looked around the room. I wasn't really being nosy. It's just that the Mann was sitting right in front of me, and looking around seemed more polite than staring at him.

From what I could see, he wasn't much of a decorator. The place was clean enough, but it didn't have any "touches," as my mom would say — no ornaments, candles, vases of flowers ... that sort of thing. There were a few pictures on the walls, but they were the kind you see in hotel rooms — pretty forgettable stuff.

I scanned the coffee table in front of the couch, searching for a magazine or even a newspaper to distract me. But all that was on it was a bowl containing about three pretzels. I was just wondering if it would be rude of me to help myself to one when the excited roar of a crowd erupted from the television, and the commentator said, "Well, that's your ball game, folks."

Then the Mann aimed the remote at the television, and the twenty thousand fans inside all of a sudden shut up.

"So what brings you fellas here?" the Mann said, putting down the footrest of the recliner. "As flattering as the thought is, I have a feeling you didn't come just to watch the game with me."

Kelly pulled a face. "Are you kidding? That game wasn't worth watching. Those two teams are so far out of the running, they'll never catch up." Then he put his hand on his neck and winced as he moved his head from side to side. "Have you ever thought about rearranging your furniture?"

The Mann glanced around the room with a *what-are-you-talking-about* expression on his face. "It looks fine to me," he said. "Besides, I don't think my living room decor is what you came about either."

Kelly shook his head. "It isn't."

The Mann sighed. "Well, that can only mean one thing. You came to tell me the score of the Demons-Lightning game."

I'd been eyeing those pretzels, but when the Mann said that, my head shot up.

"How did you know they played?" I couldn't keep the surprise out of my voice.

The Mann laughed.

"I didn't," he said. "Until just now." Then he sobered again. "And I'd be lying if I said I wasn't relieved. Thank you, boys."

"You would've found out tomorrow anyway," I pointed out.

The Mann laughed again.

"I didn't mean thank you for telling me. I meant — thank you for convincing them to play."

"We didn't." The way Kelly flung the words out, you would've thought he was looking for a fight. "I told you this morning I wouldn't do that. All we did was tell them the situation."

The Mann looked thoughtful.

"Well, thank you for that then," he said. "What about the other teams? What are they going to do?"

"I don't know," Kelly answered grudgingly. "Play, I guess. There's no reason for them to hold out now."

There was another pause, and then the Mann

asked, "Does that mean you boys will play too?"

I tensed, waiting for Kelly's answer.

He shook his head. "No. Not me."

Even though I knew Kelly was going to say that, part of me shriveled inside.

I shook my head and mumbled, "Me neither."

"Why?" the Mann exploded, and jumped out of his chair. He began marching back and forth. Finally he stopped in front of Kelly. "What do you hope to accomplish?"

Kelly looked him square in the eye. "The same thing you're accomplishing by not writing that test."

The Mann started to march some more.

"You have to play," he said.

"Why?" Kelly demanded. "Give me one good reason." It sounded like a dare.

The Mann stopped pacing. He had his back to us so I couldn't see his face. But his shoulders sagged as if he'd suddenly given up. He turned around and sank down into his recliner. Then he leaned his head against the back of the chair and stared up at the ceiling. He sat that way for so long, I started to feel real uncomfortable, like maybe the Mann had said everything he was going to, and now he was just waiting for us to leave.

In fact, I was just about to suggest we do that when he started talking again.

"Your team is scheduled to play on Thursday evening," he said in a tired voice. He was still staring at the ceiling. "A man by the name of Brian

Billings will be at that game. He is a scout for the San Francisco Giants, and he'll be expecting to see you pitch." Then he finally tore his eyes away from the ceiling and looked across at Kelly. "Is that a good enough reason for you?"

CHAPTER 15

Holy home run, Batman! I could hardly believe what the Mann was saying.

This was Kelly's dream come true! He should have been smiling his face off and bouncing off the ceiling. But instead, he was just sitting on the couch like a sack of rocks.

I decided he must have been in shock, so I punched him in the shoulder.

"Did you hear that, Kelly?" I whooped. "A scout from the Giants is coming to see you play!" Then I turned to the Mann. "Could this guy offer Kelly a contract?"

The Mann smiled and shook his head. "No, Kelly's too young for that. But if Billings likes what he sees, he could get Kelly into some good base-ball camps and help him to keep improving until he is old enough to sign."

I punched Kelly again. "This is it, man! This is exactly what you've been waiting for!"

For all the reaction I got, I might as well have been talking to a corpse. I tried again. "Now you *have* to play."

That woke him up.

"No, I don't," he said.

I think my jaw dropped onto the rug. What was wrong with him? I would've given anything to be in Kelly's shoes. This was the opportunity of a lifetime. But Kelly couldn't seem to throw it away fast enough.

"Tell me you're kidding around," I pleaded, waiting for Kelly's face to split into that familiar grin.

But it didn't.

"Don't be foolish, Kelly," the Mann took over from me. "You have a great baseball future ahead of you. Don't jeopardize it over a misplaced sense of duty. It's okay to back down. This is no time to get hung up on pride."

Kelly didn't answer.

"I mean it, Kelly," the Mann said. "Think about what you're doing. If you let this opportunity slip away, you'll regret it for the rest of your life — and so will I."

Kelly's expression became fierce. "Then write the test," he said. "If you write the test, I'll play baseball."

Now we were getting somewhere. As far as I could see, this was the perfect solution — one of those deals where everybody wins. The Mann would be umping again, we'd get to play baseball, and Kelly would move closer to his dream. But when the Mann didn't answer, I knew it wasn't going to work out that way.

"I can't," he said finally.

Since that's what he'd been saying all along, his answer wasn't really a surprise, but for some reason that I can't explain, those two little words lit a fuse inside me, and before I realized what I was doing, I'd lifted off the couch like a launched rocket.

"What is it with you two?" I exploded. "Are you in a competition to see who can be the most stubborn — or what?"

I flapped my arm at the Mann. "*You* can't write a test." Then I waved at Kelly. "*You* can't play ball. Well, baloney. Do you hear me? *Baloney*! It's all just a bunch of baloney."

I stopped and glared at them for a second. But I wasn't finished having my say, so as soon as I grabbed another breath, I lit into them again.

"I don't get it. I really don't. And it's not like I haven't tried to understand, because I have. Oh, sure, I see that the league screwed up with that test, but things have gone way past that — and you two just keep making them worse!

"And don't tell me it's the principle of the thing, because I'm not buying that one anymore either. It might've started out that way, but this little war you two have going isn't about principles anymore, and you both know it. Anyway, what good are principles if all they do is hurt people?"

I paused again. It looked like both of them were going to say something, but I didn't give them the chance.

I started with Kelly.

"You say we have to stick up for the Mann. You say he's not getting a fair deal. Fine. I hear you. But do you hear *him*? He says he wants you to play baseball! He says seeing you get a shot at the majors is more important to him than umping."

Then I turned on the Mann. "And you don't listen either! If you *really* cared about giving Kelly's dream a chance, you'd write that test, because that's what *he* wants for *you*."

I could have said a bunch more, but suddenly it dawned on me that I was telling off a grown-up, and if my parents ever found out, I'd be grounded for the rest of my life. And that was enough to start me deflating like a leaky balloon.

"Well, I guess that's all I have to say," I mumbled, and sat down.

It got real quiet. I pretended not to notice and concentrated on picking at a callus on my hand. Out of the corner of my eye, I could see Kelly staring at me. I didn't dare look across to see what the Mann was doing, but I had a feeling that if his eyes could shoot laser beams, I'd have had more holes in me than a backstop.

"That was quite a speech," the Mann said at

last. I tried to gauge how mad he was, but without seeing his face, I couldn't tell.

"Sorry," I muttered. "I guess I shouldn't have said those things."

"No, no. Don't apologize, Midge," he told me. "You obviously needed to get that off your chest. And I'm glad you did."

That made me look up. But the Mann's face didn't tell me any more than his voice had.

"Why?" I said.

"Because it helps to clear the air, and I think that's something we could all use," he replied. "Besides you made some good points." Then he smiled. "I just wish the solution was as easy as you make it sound."

"It *is* that easy," I insisted.

This time the Mann put up his hand.

"Hear me out. I am very touched by the support you boys have given me. I mean that sincerely. I know what baseball means to you both. I've seen the way you throw yourselves into the game. And to walk away from it in order to show your loyalty to me ... well, to be perfectly honest ... you surprised the pants off me. That's a heck of a sacrifice to make. Your parents must be very proud."

Whoa! No one had ever said that to me before in my entire life. I was pretty sure it was a first for Kelly too. I would've liked to think about it for a while, but the Mann was still talking, so I pushed it to the back of my mind for later.

"Midge, you said that I was more concerned with Kelly playing baseball than I was with being an umpire."

I nodded.

"Well, you are absolutely right."

"But you can have both!" I popped off again.

And again he raised his hand. "I'm getting to that," he said. Then he turned to Kelly. "You have a gift, Kelly — a wonderful gift. You can play baseball like most people can only imagine. What's even better — you love to do it. That's a combination that's pretty hard to beat, especially when it promises such a fantastic future. Don't get me wrong. Baseball isn't everything there is. If something happened today, and you could never play the game again, you wouldn't die. In fact, you'd be fine. If you get a shot at the majors and you don't make it, you'll be fine then too. But you won't be fine if you pass up your chance. This thing about me umping might seem important right now, but after a while it will fade away. Everyone will forget about it. Everyone but you, that is — if you let it get in the way of your chance to play baseball. Then, instead of it being a noble cause, all it will be is a reminder of the dream that got away. Don't let that happen. Your future is much too important."

I was all set for Kelly to start yelling again like he had in the furnace room that morning. But he surprised me.

"I want to," he said, like he was fighting with

himself, "but I keep coming back to the same thing. If you really believe what you just said, why won't you write that test?"

That had been my point all along, but I managed not to say so.

The Mann's forehead knotted up and his mouth became a tight line. Then he sighed and scratched his chin.

"It's kind of complicated, but let me see if I can explain."

I sat forward on the couch. Finally we were going to get some answers.

"When I first heard about the test," the Mann began, "I wasn't too worried. The league was making a lot of noise, but that was nothing new. The league makes noise about a lot of things. I really thought that test would blow over. But it didn't. So then I had to decide what I was going to do about it. The last thing I wanted was to give up umping." He paused. "But I knew I couldn't write that test. So I pretended it was an insult. I was hoping that with my twenty years of experience, a little indignation might do the trick, and the league would back off. At any rate, it was the only weapon I had, so I had to give it a try. Unfortunately, it wasn't enough." He shrugged. "I took my shot, and I lost. There's nothing more I can do about it."

"Yes, there is," Kelly said. "Just write the test."

The Mann shook his head. "I wish I could."

"You can!" I piped up. "It's not too late.

My dad would let you write it any time."

The Mann closed his eyes and shook his head. Then he licked his lips and began slowly. "When I say I can't write the test, boys, that's exactly what I mean. I *can't*. I can't write it, because … because … because I can't read it." He looked at us hard. "Do you understand me now? I'm not being difficult about this. I can't read."

CHAPTER 16

That's when the phone rang, and a voice inside my head said, *Saved by the bell*! Except, of course, the Mann hadn't been saved at all. He'd already confessed his secret. Whoever was calling was too late.

As the Mann reached for the phone, I looked over at Kelly. His eyes were blinking like they were trying to jump-start his brain. I knew exactly how he felt, because I was in shock too.

How could the Mann not know how to read? He was a grown-up. He worked in a school, for Pete's sake!

I mean, it's not like he was too dumb to have learned. The Mann was smart — really smart! In fact, he was one of the smartest people I'd ever met.

But he couldn't read. That idea just didn't seem to want to get into my head.

I glanced around the room, almost like I hadn't seen it before. It looked different. It hadn't magically changed or anything, but now — instead of noticing how it was decorated — all I could see was that there were no books in it. Not one. Not anywhere. And suddenly a little part of me knew that the Mann was telling the truth.

He really couldn't read.

I'm not the world's biggest book fan myself, so I'm not criticizing. But I do know how to read. It's one of those things you learn in first grade, and from then on, you do it without even thinking — kind of like breathing. While you sit at the table eating breakfast and trying to wake up, you find yourself reading the cereal box. While you're riding the bus, you read billboards and the signs in shop windows. You read notices on lampposts, and the songs on CD covers. Schedules, maps, the telephone book, medicine bottles, flyers, brochures — every time you turn around, you have to read something. It's part of life.

So if that was true, how had the Mann survived all this time without being able to do it? In his job he must've had to fill out reports and stuff. And it only made sense that if he couldn't read, he wouldn't be able to write either.

The more I thought about the situation, the more I began to realize what a huge problem it was. The thing is, not only had the Mann handled the problem, but he'd done it without anyone finding out. And that was amazing.

"Actually, I am a little busy at the moment," he was saying to the person on the other end of the phone. "Would it be all right if I called you back?" Pause. "Good. Thanks, Edna. I'll talk to you in a little while."

Edna!

That was Mrs. Butterman! Mrs. Butterman was calling the Mann at his home! That was even worse than finding out the Mann couldn't read!

He put the phone back down on the table beside his chair and started talking again as if he'd never been interrupted. "So you see, boys, when I said I couldn't write that test, I really couldn't."

"Why didn't you tell us that in the first place?" Kelly said.

"Isn't it obvious?" the Mann replied quietly. "It's not the sort of thing a person wants to advertise. I was embarrassed and ashamed." He lowered his eyes. "I still am. I wouldn't be telling you now if it wasn't for this boycott." Then he looked up again. "But if it gets you back on the baseball field, the humiliation will be worth it. So … will you play?"

If it had just been me, I would've jumped off the couch right then and yelled, *You betcha! Absolutely. Of course, I'll play.* But this was between Kelly and the Mann, so I stuck my tongue between my teeth and mentally crossed my fingers as I waited for Kelly's answer.

When a minute went by and he didn't say anything, I began to wonder if he'd heard the question.

The Mann must've been thinking the same thing because he repeated it.

"Will you play?"

"Why *can't* you read?" Kelly shot back. "How come you never learned? Didn't you go to school?"

The Mann looked surprised. "Of course, I did," he said. Then he glanced self-consciously toward his feet. "I just didn't — " Then he blurted, "Look, you fellas don't want to hear this. It isn't that interesting a story."

"Tell us anyway," Kelly said.

I have to admit that I was curious too, but the Mann didn't look like he was real comfortable with the subject.

"Maybe he doesn't want to talk about it, Kel," I said.

But Kelly didn't take the hint. "Is it a medical thing — you know, like a learning disability or something?"

The Mann shook his head. "No. Nothing like that. It was just one of those things that happened — or should I say, *didn't* happen." He offered us a weak smile. Then his eyes moved back and forth between Kelly and me. Finally he said, "You're not going to let me off the hook here, are you?"

Neither Kelly nor I answered. I guess we didn't need to, because after a while the Mann started telling us his story.

"Looking back, it all seems so senseless now," he sighed. "There was no good reason I shouldn't have learned to read. I wasn't a stupid kid. In fact, my teachers said I had a very active mind." He snickered wryly. "Unfortunately, I had an even more active body. I just couldn't sit still, and being stuck in a desk all day long was sheer torture for me. With the sun streaming through the classroom window, all I could think about was getting outside to play. I couldn't have been more of a prisoner if I'd been locked away in a castle dungeon. As far as I was concerned, the only good part of school was recess!"

He smiled at his own joke before continuing.

"Books just didn't do it for me. I didn't mind it so much when the teacher read and all I had to do was listen, but trying to make sense of all those letters myself was just too slow a process. I didn't have the patience for it. So by the end of first grade, I hadn't learned to do much more than write my name.

"And then I discovered baseball, and things at school went from bad to worse. There was only room in my head for one thing — and it sure as heck wasn't reading."

He peered through his eyebrows at Kelly. "I was a pitcher ... like you. And the only place I wanted to be was on the ball field. As far as I was concerned there was nowhere else!

"My teachers tried. I'll give them that. They gave me extra help, kept me after school, had conferences with my parents, even held me back a year." He shrugged. "None of it did any good.

The better I got at baseball, the less effort I put into my schoolwork. Eventually, I guess, my teachers must have given up too, and I just kind of slipped through the cracks."

The leather of the recliner squeaked and groaned as the Mann shifted his position. When he was comfortable, he carried on with his story.

"But you see, it didn't matter," he said with a glint in his eye, "because by the time I reached my teens, I'd already decided I didn't need school. I was going to be a professional baseball player." The Mann shook his head at the memory and chuckled. "I wish I was as smart now as I thought I was back then."

Then he sobered again and shook a finger at us. "Don't get me wrong. I had talent — plenty of it."

He looked at Kelly again. "Maybe not so much as you, but enough to make me think I could make it in the big leagues." He shrugged. "And you never know, I might have — if I hadn't had that accident."

"What accident?" Kelly and I asked at the same time.

The Mann opened his mouth, and then shut it. He raised a hand. "One thing first. I want to make sure you understand that I'm not proud of this next bit. You got it?"

Kelly and I nodded.

"Okay. Good. Just make sure you remember that." The Mann took another deep breath and resumed his story. "A buddy and I went for a joy ride in his father's car. He had his license, but I didn't. That would have involved writing a test for the learner's permit, which I couldn't do. Of course, my friend didn't know that was the reason I couldn't drive. He thought it was because my folks didn't want me to.

"Anyway, this particular day he decided to give me a lesson and … well, I'm sure you can guess the rest. We smashed up the car and my arm too — my pitching arm."

I was so caught up in the Mann's story I gasped out loud at that, and both Kelly and the Mann turned to look at me.

"It's okay, Midge." The Mann grinned and gave his arm a shake. "It took a while, but eventually the arm was as good as new — except for the pitching. That was never the same again, and in the few seconds it had taken to crash that car," he snapped his fingers, "my dreams of playing professional ball were finished."

We were all quiet for a minute, and then Kelly asked, "So what did you do then?"

The Mann leaned his head back against the recliner.

"For a while, nothing. Just felt sorry for myself, mostly. I was still going to school — though I don't know why. I certainly wasn't learning anything. But it was someplace to go. And if I didn't disrupt the class, teachers tolerated me. So I just drifted to a desk at the back and pretended I was invisible. The thing is, as I sat there an interesting thing started to happen."

Kelly and I both leaned forward.

"What?"

The Mann grinned.

"I began to listen," he said. Then he spread his hands apologetically. "It was probably the first time in my life I'd actually sat still long enough to pay attention. And what I discovered is that I liked what I was hearing. I was learning things. I was learning about science and history, geography, and math. I was learning about people and government and world events.

"And it got me excited. I didn't know how to read, but that didn't mean I couldn't learn other ways. And so I did. I began learning everything I could, any way I could get the information. I listened to people talk. I listened to the radio. I watched television. I watched people do things. I checked talking books out of the library, so I could catch up on the literature I'd missed. I went to plays and concerts, lectures, and sporting events. With my own educational system underway, there didn't seem much point staying in school anymore, so I dropped out and started traveling, taking any job I could get — for the money, but also for the education. I worked on a fishing boat, in construction, in a nursery, at a sawmill, in a bakery, for a mechanic, and on an oil rig. By the time I was twenty-five,

I had to have had thirty different jobs.

"Even so, I still couldn't get baseball out of my system. I needed to find some way to be a part of the game. If I couldn't be a player, perhaps I could be involved in a different way — as a high school or college coach, maybe. It didn't take long to realize that wasn't an option for me either. Without a university education, no one would even look at me. Not learning to read and dropping out of school had really messed up my future. Umping minor league ball was the best I could do."

"How did you end up being a custodian?" I asked.

The Mann shrugged. "I just sort of fell into that one. I was in the right place at the right time, and I had the skills that were needed." He smiled. "Well, most of them, anyway. I faked the rest."

"Has anyone ever found out you can't read?" Kelly asked.

"Some people have suspected, I think," he admitted, "but no one has ever come straight out and asked me, and I certainly haven't volunteered the information — until now."

"Wow," I said.

Then the Mann's face went all serious.

"Don't get the impression that what I've done is glamorous," he said sternly. "Because it isn't. It was darn hard work, and if I had my life to live over, I would definitely make better use of my schooling. The only reason I'm telling you this at all is so that you boys will learn from my mistakes, *and* that you will play baseball on Thursday night. So, what do you say? Will you play?"

I looked at Kelly. After all the Mann had told us, I didn't see how he could possibly say no. But one look at his face, and I began to have doubts again.

At last he nodded. "Yeah," he said. "We'll play."

The Mann's face broke into a grin that reminded me of Kelly's, and then, just as quickly, he sobered again.

"There's one more thing."

Kelly and I both looked at him.

"I'm still not anxious for the rest of the world to know about this reading thing," he said, "so I'd appreciate it if you boys would keep what I told you under your hats."

CHAPTER 17

When we left the Mann's house, I felt more light-hearted than I had in a week. It looked like things were finally getting back on track. The boycotts were over, and we were going to start playing base-ball again. And best of all, a major league scout was coming to watch Kelly pitch.

On the way home, I treated us both to a beer — a root beer, that is — to celebrate.

"Here's to Cairo Kelly's future in the majors, and to the great seats he is going to get for his best friend," I said, raising my drink.

Kelly rolled his eyes. "How about here's to our chances of winning the championship?" he countered.

"I'll drink to that too," I grinned, and we clinked cans.

After a long guzzle, Kelly wiped his mouth on his hand.

"Thanks, Midge," he said. "I needed that."

I let out a huge sigh. "Me too. I can't believe how stressed I've been. If this is what it's like to be a grown-up, then I'm gonna stay a kid forever."

Kelly's eyebrows shot up. "You really want to be in seventh grade for the rest of your life?"

A picture of Miss Drummond flashed through my mind, and I shuddered. "Okay, so maybe I need to give it some more thought."

Kelly laughed, and I realized how long it had been since he'd done that. At the risk of spoiling the mood, I said, "I'm glad you told the Mann you'd play."

His laugh died.

Obviously this was still a touchy subject. At first I thought it was because Kelly wasn't over being stubborn yet, but then I remembered thinking the same thing about the Mann. And look how wrong I'd been about that! No, there had to be some other reason Kelly was acting strange. And I was pretty sure it had to do with the Mann.

"Can I ask you something, Kel?" I said, and then before he could say no, I plunged on. "Actually it's two things. One — how did you know where the Mann's house was? And two — why did you call him by his first name?"

I'd expected Kelly to avoid answering my questions, but he didn't.

"Because he's my big brother," he replied so fast that it took me a few seconds to realize what he'd said.

When I did, my mouth opened and shut a few

times before I actually managed to get any words to come out of it. "He's your ... your ... he's your brother!" I stammered. *Wow*! The thought was mind-boggling! But as I tried to get my head around the idea, I had another thought. "Hey — wait a second," I said. "There's no way the Mann could be your brother. He's older than your mom!"

"He's not my *brother*, you moron," Kelly smirked. "He's my *Big* Brother. You know — as in *The Big Brothers?* Men who do stuff with boys who don't have fathers?"

"Oh," I said, suddenly feeling stupid. Then I frowned. "Why didn't you say that in the first place? How long has he been your ... " It felt funny saying the words. " ... your Big Brother?"

Kelly made an *I-don't-know* face. "I think I was nine, so it's been about four years, I guess."

"Four years!" I exclaimed. "You and the Mann have been hanging out for four years? And you never said anything to me?"

"Don't get bent out of shape about it," Kelly said. "It's not that big a deal. Every couple of weeks we go to a movie, maybe play some catch or grab a hamburger — you know, stuff like that. Nothing major. Besides, it was my mom's idea. After she watched some program on juvenile delinquency, she decided I needed a male role model in my life and signed me up. "

"Is that why you can't hang out some Saturdays?" He nodded.

"So, what do you and the Mann talk about?"

He frowned. "I don't know — stuff. I don't keep a diary."

"What kind of stuff? Baseball? School? Movies?"

He nodded. "Yeah, that and, like, what kind of kisser Babe Ruth is."

My mouth dropped open. "You've kissed Babe Ruth!"

Kelly burst out laughing and slapped his knee. "Man, you're gullible. No, I haven't kissed her." Then he waggled his eyebrows a couple of times. "Not yet, anyway. I'm saving that for when baseball season's over. But I doubt that I'll be sharing the details with the Mann."

We were quiet for a couple of minutes. Then I said, "How come you never told me?"

"About Babe Ruth?" Kelly laughed again.

I gave him a shove. "No, you jerk. About the Mann."

"You mean about him being my Big Brother?"

I nodded.

Kelly shrugged. "Maybe for the same reason he didn't tell us he couldn't read. It would make everything different. You would have felt different about him *and* me, and I didn't want that."

I was all set to argue the point, but for once my brain kicked in before my mouth started flapping. And I realized he was right, because I already felt different, and I hadn't even known about the two of them for five minutes.

Kelly and the Mann had been spending every other Saturday together for the past four years, so it only made sense that Kelly knew the Mann better than I did. You can't spend that much time with someone without getting to know him. Kelly even called the Mann by his first name. In an adult-kid kind of way, they were probably friends.

It was weird thinking of Kelly and the Mann like that, but at least it explained a few things — like Kelly's determination to get the Mann's umping job back, for instance. The other guys and I were willing to risk our baseball season to help the Mann, and we only knew him as an umpire, but if Kelly had been hanging out with him for four years, he must have had way stronger feelings than that.

He probably knew how much umping meant to the Mann. And that's why he was so determined to get him back doing it. And the Mann really cared about Kelly too. He told us a secret he'd kept all his life, just so Kelly wouldn't throw away a shot at the majors.

Suddenly I felt guilty about the way I had accused them both of being stubborn.

"That was a pretty nice thing the Mann did for you, Kel," I said. "It was good what you tried to do for him too. I really wish we could've found a way around that test."

Kelly looked like his mind was a million miles away, so I was surprised when he answered me.

"Yeah," he said. "So do I."

CHAPTER 18

The idea came to me later that evening, halfway through a rerun of *Star Trek Voyager*. I'd seen the episode before, so I guess my mind was wandering a bit. All I know is that one second I was watching Captain Janeway and Seven arguing about turning an intergalactic criminal over to the authorities of some planet, and the next second I'd figured out how to get the Mann umping again.

The solution was so simple, I couldn't understand why I hadn't thought of it before. Of course, if the scheme was going to work, the Mann would have to cooperate, but I'd let Kelly worry about that part.

I was so pumped, I wanted to phone him right that minute, but I couldn't risk my parents overhearing our conversation. If they found out what I had in mind, my plan would be finished before it even began.

"Midge, it's time for bed."

I looked at my watch. Mom was right on schedule.

I changed into my PJs without arguing and headed to the bathroom. Then I squeezed a blob of toothpaste onto my brush and began cleaning my teeth. Five minutes later, I was still brushing — and planning.

Mom knocked on the bathroom door. "Don't forget to floss," she said.

"I won't," I called back.

That night I didn't just tear off a hunk of floss and chuck it into the wastebasket like I usually do. I actually used it. It's not that I was suddenly worried about cavities or anything; I was just killing time until my parents went to bed, so that I could carry out the first part of my plan. Hopefully, they wouldn't keep me waiting long. Not that I was all that worried. My parents' idea of a late night is watching the eleven o'clock news, but most nights they're lucky to make it to ten-thirty. I crossed my fingers that this was one of those nights.

At ten past ten, Mom noticed that I was still up and got on my case again, so I headed to my room. Then I remembered about the flashlight and detoured to the kitchen to get it. But Dad was there, making himself a peanut butter sandwich, so instead of going to the drawer where the flashlight is kept, I opened the fridge and stuck my head inside for a look.

"Didn't you just do your teeth?" Dad asked.

"Yeah," I replied as I peeked under the lid of a plastic container.

"Well then, get out of there," he said. "If you have something to eat, you'll have to brush all over again."

Mom wandered in. She was already in her dressing gown.

"What are you still doing up?" She frowned at me. "You're supposed to be in bed."

"I'm goin'," I grumbled. Then I had a brainwave. "Has anybody seen the measuring tape?"

"Not in the fridge," Mom said sarcastically.

"What measuring tape?" Dad asked.

"You know — the metal one that retracts."

"It's in the junk drawer." Mom pointed absently toward the kitchen drawer where we keep everything from toothpicks to tire patches. When I was a little kid I could spend hours doing nothing but rooting through that drawer. "Why?" she added. "What do you want with that old tape measure?"

I headed for the drawer.

"It's for math class tomorrow. Mr. Pugh is going to have us measure stuff and then work out the perimeter and area. He asked people to bring in tape measures if they can." It was a lie, but because it was for a good cause, I told myself it didn't really count.

I dragged open the drawer and began rummaging around inside, making sure to keep my body between the drawer and my parents. I spotted the flashlight right away and stuffed it into the waist-band of my PJs. Then I hunted around some more until I found the tape measure.

"I got it," I beamed, holding it up for my parents to see. Then I closed the drawer. "Well, I guess I better hit the hay. G'night."

I don't know how long I lay in bed, waiting for my parents to settle down for the night, but it felt like ages. I even dozed off once, but the sound of the toilet flushing worked its way into the dream I was having about falling into a waterfall, and my body jerked me awake again.

I propped myself up on one elbow and peered toward the door. There was no light showing. I went to push the covers off, but then I heard something and grabbed them back up to my chin and quickly closed my eyes again. I listened hard, but I couldn't hear anything except my own heart pounding. After a while it finally quieted down enough for me to recognize the noise that had scared me. It was my dad snoring.

I reached under my pillow for the flashlight and slid out of bed. I hadn't shut my bedroom door completely, so I pulled it open without turning the handle, and peeked out. The night light in the bathroom cast weird shadows along the hallway, but at least I could see without switching on the flashlight. My parents' door was closed and from behind it — louder than ever here in the hall

— came the rumbling of my dad's snoring.

I took that as a good sign and began tiptoeing toward the study on the other side of my parents' room. But right in front of their door, a floorboard squeaked so loudly that you would've thought I'd stepped on a cat's tail — which is a bit tricky, since we don't have a cat. Instantly the snoring stopped, and so did I. Holding my breath, I listened for feet to come charging into the hall with my dad attached to them. But then the snoring started up again. Without wasting another second, I hurried past and into the study.

I eased the door shut and flicked on the flashlight. I wanted to get this over with and get back to my own room as fast as I could. I shone the light onto my dad's desk. Except for the computer and a mug filled with pens and pencils, it was empty, which meant I was going to have to go through my dad's filing cabinet. *Darn*!

I flashed the light in that direction and sent a bunch of prayers up to God. Please don't let the filing cabinet be locked. Please make the drawer not squeak. Please let Dad's umpire stuff be in there. Of course, why God would want to help me carry out a burglary, I didn't know, but I was hoping He would take into consideration the circumstances — and besides, what harm could it do to ask?

I clenched my teeth and pulled on the drawer. It moved. It wasn't locked. *Whew*! That was a start.

If God wasn't helping me, at least He didn't seem to be working against me. I pulled the drawer open all the way. No squeak. I cast my eyes toward the ceiling.

Thank you, I mouthed the words.

Then I took a deep breath. Now all I had to do was find the right folder. I could tell by glancing at the tabs that everything was filed alphabetically. That was a help. The only question was — *what would Dad have filed it under*?

Baseball? No, not there.

Umpiring? My fingers flipped through the hanging folders. Yes! There it was.

Then my hopes fell again. The folder had to be three inches thick, with a whole bunch of smaller folders stuffed inside the big one. This could take me all night!

I placed the flashlight on top of the files so that it was shining on the umpire folder. Then, using both hands, I began riffling through the papers inside. Dad must have put the newest stuff at the front, because I found what I was looking for almost right away.

I slid the stapled sheets out of the folder and shone the flashlight on them. This was it — *Hampshire Park District Minor League Baseball Comprehensive Umpire Examination*. It was all there — four pages, thirty multiple-choice questions.

I rolled the drawer shut as quietly as I could

and stuffed the test under my pajama top, just in case I ran into anyone on my return trip down the hall. Then I switched off the flashlight, opened the study door and — after making sure the coast was clear — hurried back to my room.

CHAPTER 19

The Mann agreed to meet us in the furnace room after school.

"Absolutely not!" he exploded, when we explained what we wanted to do. "Forget it. There is no way — *no way*! I can't believe you are even suggesting such a thing."

"Why not?" Kelly demanded.

The Mann had been pacing, but he stopped in mid-stride and looked at Kelly as if his brain had fallen onto the floor.

"Why not?" he repeated. Then he shook his head. "Are you serious? Does the word *dishonest* ring any bells at all?"

"But it *isn't* dishonest," I protested, and then when the Mann turned his glare on me, I added more quietly, " Well, not completely. I mean, I guess it's sort of dishonest, but… "

"*Sort of*?" the Mann cut me off. "How can something be *sort of* dishonest? Either it is, or it isn't."

"Okay, fine — it's dishonest," I conceded, "but it's not really cheating. We wouldn't be giving you the answers — just the questions."

"And that's supposed to make it okay?" the Mann roared.

"Think of it this way," Kelly said. "It would be like taking the test orally. Really, that's all you'd be doing. We ask you the questions, and you choose the correct answer from the multiple choices. Midge and I write down the letters of the answers you want, and you memorize them in order. That'll be a snap for you. Then when you take the real test, all you have to do is circle the answers that you memorized."

"It isn't cheating," I emphasized again, "because you won't get a chance to check anywhere to see if your answers are right."

"You can dress it up any way you like, it's still cheating," the Mann grumbled, but he was definitely calmer.

I had an idea.

"Let's say you told my dad that you couldn't read," I said, and a look of shock flooded the Mann's face. "I'm not suggesting you actually *tell* him that," I backtracked quickly. "I'm just saying *what if*. Anyway, if you told him you couldn't read, and he offered to read the questions to you, would that be cheating?"

"Of course not," he said.

"Well, there you go," Kelly grinned. "This is exactly the same thing."

"With one noteworthy difference," the Mann scowled. "It isn't Midge's dad asking me the questions. It's you two."

"The thing is, he *would* ask you the questions if he knew you couldn't read," I insisted. "It's just that you don't want to tell him." And then I added, "And we promised we wouldn't. So you see — really, Kelly and I are performing a community service."

"That's right," Kelly agreed.

The Mann shut his eyes and shook his head. "Only you two could come up with that kind of convoluted logic."

I was pretty sure the Mann was weakening, but he wasn't quite there yet. We needed something to push him over the top.

"You said yesterday that you wished you could write the test," I told him. "You said the reason you didn't do it before was because you couldn't read, and you didn't want anyone to find that out. Isn't that right?"

"Yes," the Mann replied reluctantly, "but — "

"Well, we're offering you a solution that takes care of all those problems," I beamed. "You can write the test without anyone finding out you can't read, and then you'll be able to ump again. Isn't that what you want?"

"Well, yes," the Mann said again, "but …"

"Then there's absolutely no excuse for you to hold out now ..." I paused for emphasis "... except stubbornness."

The Mann pointed a finger at me. "That was a low blow."

I shrugged.

"Anyway," Kelly attacked him from the other side, "don't you think you owe it to all the guys on the teams? They risked everything to get you back umping. Think about them."

The Mann looked hard at Kelly, but he didn't say anything, and Kelly came in for the knockout punch.

"If you won't do it for yourself or the ball players," he said, "then do it for me. I want to see you umping again about as much as you want me to have a shot at the majors."

"Just two more to go," I said, flipping onto the last page. "Are you ready?"

"Go ahead," the Mann sighed.

"Okay. Number twenty-nine. Complete this statement correctly. The infield fly rule comes into effect when: A – the bases are loaded and there are no outs; B – the batter has two strikes and there are two or more runners on base; C – there are two batters out and two or more runners on base; or D – the count is full and the bases are loaded."

"The bases are loaded and there are no outs," the Mann said.

I looked at Kelly. "That's A," I told him.

"Number twenty-nine is A," he said, writing it down.

I looked back at the test. "This is the last one. Which of the following is *not* a balk? Here are the choices: A – when the pitcher does not pause in his windup before delivering the ball; B – when the pitcher moves his shoulder or leg toward first base during his windup but completes the pitch to the plate; C – when there are runners at the corners, and the pitcher fakes a throw to third base; and D – when the pitcher's foot is not in contact with the rubber at the beginning of his windup."

"You should know this one, Kelly," the Mann said.

"I do," Kelly nodded, "but I'm not the person who has to answer it."

"You're no fun," the Mann harumphed, and then turned to me. "It's the third one, Midge. It isn't a balk when there are runners at the corners, and the pitcher fakes a throw to third base."

"Number thirty is C," I said.

"Thirty is C." Kelly recorded the answer. Then he looked up and grinned. "And that's it. No more questions. Now you're all set to take this test, Hal. I've written the A, B, C, D answers so that the letters look just like on the test. All you have to do is memorize the order, and call Midge's dad tonight so you can take the test tomorrow."

"And remember — when you're doing the test,

take a little time with each question so that it looks like you're actually reading them," I reminded him. "If you circle all the answers in, like, thirty seconds, my dad might get a little suspicious."

The Mann frowned. "I still don't like this."

"You can't back out now," Kelly told him. "Just memorize the order and phone Mr. Ridge." He grabbed his books off the desk and opened the door before the Mann could say anything else. "Now we gotta get going. Midge has to return that test, and then we have baseball practice. See ya tomorrow."

"See ya," I echoed, closing the door.

A few steps down the hall, Kelly spun around like he'd just remembered something, jogged back to the furnace room and stuck his head around the door.

"Oh, and Hal," he grinned, "don't study too hard, eh?"

CHAPTER 20

Practice went great. Even though it had been less than a week since our last game, it felt more like we'd been off all winter, and everybody was as itchy to play as if it was the beginning of a new season.

We were all there, grinning and laughing, swinging bats and pounding the pockets of our mitts. Even Coach Bryant was in a good mood. He didn't say a single word about the protests either. But that didn't stop him from working us hard — not that anybody minded. We all knew what was at stake, and none of us wanted our season to end.

Kelly and I didn't leave with the other guys when practice was over. We just weren't ready to call it a night. We hadn't swung at enough pitches. We hadn't scooped up enough grounders. We hadn't felt the ball thwack into our gloves enough times. We were still hungry to play.

And with the scout from the Giants coming to

Thursday's game, Kelly needed to pitch. It wasn't that he was rusty after a week's layoff; it had more to do with getting his head into the right space.

I'm no catcher, but I am Kelly's best friend — and I'm pretty sure he wouldn't kill me on purpose — so I hunkered down behind home plate and held up my glove for him to throw at. Kelly took his place on the mound and wound up just like it was a real game and the stands were filled with fans. And then he went through every pitch in his repertoire.

But like I said, I'm not a catcher, and after twenty minutes of Kelly throwing smoke, my hand was on fire. I stood up and pulled off my glove. My palm looked like raw hamburger meat.

"Have you had enough?" Kelly called as he headed in from the mound.

"Are you kidding?" I waved my hand in the air to cool it off. "I had enough about twenty pitches ago."

Kelly shook his head and grinned. "You're outta shape, Midge."

"What are you talking about?" I retorted. "I'd like to see *you* catch the stuff that you throw!"

He shrugged. "Pete does it all the time."

"Yeah — with a catcher's mitt! In case you haven't noticed, that's got a whole lot more padding than this!" I said, chucking my glove at him.

Naturally he chucked it right back, and so we spent the next couple of minutes clobbering each other with our gloves and raising the dust around home plate.

When we were finally exhausted, we wandered over to the dugout and collapsed onto the bench inside.

"Are you nervous about Thursday's game?" I asked after a while.

"Just when I think about it," Kelly said. Then he grinned and added, "Which is only all the time."

I nodded. "Maybe that's why the Mann didn't want to tell you about that scout."

"Could be," he agreed. "He's pretty smart about that kind of stuff."

That and just about everything else, I thought to myself. In fact, he seemed to have all kinds of information nobody else had. I frowned. "How do you think the Mann knew — about Coach Billings coming to the game, I mean?"

Kelly shook his head. "Beats me."

"Do you think maybe Coach Bryant told him?"

Kelly considered that for a minute. "Nah, I don't think so. To tell you the truth, I don't think Coach even knows about it. I'm pretty sure he would have said something if he did."

"Yeah, I guess," I agreed. Then I said, "Anyway, the important thing is not to think too much about this scout. Just play your game. You'll be great."

Kelly let out a sigh. "Thanks. I'll try. The thing is …" He paused, and then he shook his head. "Never mind. It doesn't matter."

"What were you going to say?"

"Nothing. It's all right."

"Kelly," I urged him, "we're friends. If something is bugging you, get it off your chest."

He looked at me, and then he looked back out toward the diamond.

"It's just that I really, really want this, Midge. And that scares the heck out of me, because if I don't get it, I'll have less than I had before." He turned to look at me again. "Do you know what I mean?"

I could tell from the expression on Kelly's face that it was important to him that I understand. The thing is, I wasn't sure that I did. Having a major league scout come to check him out was huge. That part I understood. And I'll admit I was a bit jealous — okay, fine — I was a *lot* jealous! What guy wouldn't be? But I still wanted things to work out for Kelly.

"Is it like what the Mann said about living the dream?" I asked.

Kelly's face relaxed a little. He nodded. "Yeah. Yeah, sort of."

I thought about that a little bit more, and then Kelly said, "All my life, I've felt like everybody else was better than me. And the thing is, it's because of stuff I didn't have any control over — like my mother not speaking English very well, and like her working as a maid because she doesn't have enough education to get any other job. It doesn't matter that she works harder than three people rolled into one. All anybody sees when they look at her is an ignorant immigrant.

"And since hotel maids don't make a pile of

money, we're poor, and there's nothing that makes you an outsider faster than having no money. Most kids at our school live in big houses with two-and three-car garages. They have computers, all the latest designer clothes, enough CDs to start their own stores, and they vacation in Florida or California every year. Me and Ma live in a crummy apartment, and we can barely afford that. We don't have a car, we don't have a computer, we don't have a CD player, and in my whole life, we've never gone on a holiday anywhere.

"The thing is, it's always been that way. I don't blame my mother. I know she's doing the best she can. But that doesn't mean the situation doesn't bother me. I just pretend that it doesn't. And I tell myself that someday when I'm an adult, things will be different." He kind of half-smiled. "Of course, what I'm going to do to make them different, I've never quite gotten around to figuring out."

His face became serious again. "At least, not until Skylar Hogue wrote that article. That's what made a difference. When *Sport Beat* magazine came out with me in it, it was like a sky that had been nothing but black clouds my entire life was suddenly showing a patch of blue. And that's when I knew that I really could change things. I didn't have to pretend anymore."

I was Kelly's best friend, but until that minute I'd never known how he felt about himself. Every guy in the school wanted to be like Kelly, and every girl wanted Kelly for her boyfriend. But what Kelly wanted was to be like everybody else. Miss Drummond would have said that was ironic.

I scratched my head.

"I know you'll probably think this is crazy," I said, "but this sounds like one of those grass is greener on the other side of the fence deals. You sabotage the system every chance you get, but what you really want is to fit into it. And all the kids who live the life you want would give anything to be like you. Everybody wants what the other guy's got.

"But think about it. So you don't have money right now. I know it's no fun, but look at what you *do* have. You can play baseball. And all those guys with CDs can't. Would you really want to trade? Besides, the only reason things are how they are anyway is because your dad was killed in that ship-wreck. If it wasn't for that, your mom and him would've gotten married and you'd be just like everybody else."

Kelly chewed on his lip and then shook his head.

"That's another one of those things I pretended about," he said. "My dad isn't dead."

I sat right up. "Say what?"

"He's not dead," Kelly repeated. "Though he might as well be. In fact, I'm pretty sure Ma wishes he was. He's in prison somewhere for stealing. And it isn't the first time either. As fast as they let him out, he steals something else, and he's back in again."

"Your dad?"

Kelly snorted. "Yeah — *my dad*. I've never met the guy. I haven't even seen a picture of him. Just mentioning him sends Ma into a fit. He phoned her once — between stints in prison — and she was so upset, she couldn't speak English for three days."

"So then, your parents *are* married?"

Kelly shook his head. "No. That part is true. But it isn't quite as romantic as I made it sound. My dad wasn't a sailor. He wasn't even Egyptian. He was just some guy who loaded and unloaded ships in the harbor. But him and a ship called the *Cairo Queen* were the first things Ma laid eyes on when she and Gramps landed here from Italy. That's where I got the idea for the nickname.

"Anyway, my dad saw Ma too. She was just sixteen and pretty — I've seen pictures — and about as naive as they come." He turned to me and spread his hands. "I'm living proof of that."

Something about this whole thing puzzled me.

"If your dad is such bad news, why the nickname? Isn't it just a reminder of what a creep he is?"

Kelly shrugged. "For my mom, I guess it is, but according to my grandfather, I'm reminder enough. He says I look exactly like my father. I think that's why Ma is always on my case about staying out of trouble and getting an education. She's afraid I'm going to end up like him. She thinks being a dreamer is what made him a crook." He paused. "But I think it's exactly the opposite. Maybe if he'd had a dream, he would've been all right."

CHAPTER 21

I thought about that conversation all the way home.

Lately Kelly had been full of surprises. He was friends with the Mann. He envied other kids. And he had a dad. *Wow*! Kelly had a dad!

Well, sort of, I decided more realistically. A picture of my own dad popped into my head, and something warm — like the feeling you get when you put on a shirt straight from the dryer — rolled over me. It was there and gone so fast, I couldn't really say what it was, but I knew it had to do with my dad. I'd never given it much thought before, but at that moment I was glad I had the parents I had. They could be a pain sometimes, but at least they were there, and I knew I could count on them.

Not like Kelly's dad. The guy sounded like a major loser. It was no wonder Kelly had made up a story about him. Who needed a father like that?

Kelly was better off without him.

Besides, Kelly had the Mann, and it seemed to me that he was way more of a father to Kelly than his real dad was anyway. They might not be related, but they did stuff together, and they cared about each other. And wasn't that what really counted?

Naturally, that got me thinking about the Mann again and wondering if he'd called my dad about the test. And suddenly I couldn't wait to find out.

Mom was sitting at the kitchen table when I ran into the house. She looked up from the magazine she was reading.

"How was practice?"

"Good," I answered, only half paying attention. I was more interested in locating my dad.

Mom glanced at her watch. "It went long," she said.

"Kelly and I stayed after," I told her. "Where's Dad?"

"Watching television." Then she looked at me funny. "Why? Is something wrong?"

Oops! My eagerness to find out about the Mann must have been showing. I was going to have to get myself under control. Making my parents suspicious was the last thing I wanted to do.

"No." I faked a nonchalant shrug and headed for the fridge. "Nothing's wrong. I was just asking."

Bending over, I opened the fruit keeper and started picking through the apples to find one that wasn't bruised — and to buy some time while I got myself calmed down.

That's when my dad walked in. He reached over the top of me and grabbed the orange juice container.

"Hey, guy," he said. "I didn't know you were home. How'd practice go?"

"Good," I said, keeping my head lowered. I didn't want him to see my face, in case it was doing something it shouldn't be.

"It went a little late, didn't it?" he asked.

This time I did look up.

"Are you and Mom working with one brain?" I frowned. "She just asked me the same thing."

"Great minds think alike," he recited one of his many sayings. He was obviously in a good mood. He raised the juice carton to his mouth, but when my mother made a big production of clearing her throat, he poured some into a glass instead. Then he leaned against the counter and crossed his arms over his chest. "Guess who called me tonight?" he said.

I would have bet the district championship I knew the answer to that one, but I shook my head and bit into my apple instead.

"Hal Mann," he grinned, not even trying to draw out the suspense.

"Oh, yeah?" I said, and took another bite of my apple. "What did he want?"

Dad's grin got bigger. "He wants to write the test."

I acted surprised. "You're kidding!"

"Nope. He said he's had a change of heart. All the support you kids gave him must have gotten to him."

"Wow!" I said. "That's great. So when is this gonna happen?"

"Tomorrow night. I'm umping tomorrow night's game, but I'm going to meet him at the community center after that."

I nodded. And then I asked the question I really wanted the answer to. "If he passes, will he be doing my game on Thursday?"

Dad looked unsure. "The schedule is already made up."

"Yeah, but you could change it, couldn't you? Think what it would mean to everyone," I pointed out. "All the mess over the playoffs was because of that test. Don't you think it would make everybody feel better if they knew it hadn't been for nothing? Seeing the Mann behind the plate again would do that."

"I suppose," Dad conceded skeptically.

"Then you'll change the schedule?" I pushed.

"We'll see," he said, and I knew from experience that that was as much commitment as I was going to get.

After school the next day, Kelly and I quizzed the Mann on his answers. He knew them cold. He was ready. So we wished him luck and crossed our fingers. The rest was up to him. All Kelly and I could do now was wait.

And that killed!

The evening was so long, I could barely stand it. I went to the Panthers-Whips game, but I wasn't into it. I should have been, because if we won our game, we'd have to face the winner of theirs. But the only thing I could think about was the Mann and that test he was going to write.

All I wanted was for the game to be over, so the test could be over too. No such luck. The game went into extra innings. In fact, it was starting to get dark before the Whips finally sneaked in a run to take the victory.

And as soon as that winning run crossed home plate, my eyes were on my dad, willing him to get into his car and drive to the community center.

The test must have taken a long time, because Dad didn't get home until way after I'd gone to bed. When I heard him come in, I wanted to tear out to the living room to find out how the test had gone, but I knew that would make me seem too anxious. So I forced myself to stay put, and strained my ears to see if I could learn anything that way.

My parents were talking, but their voices were lowered, and I could only catch the occasional word — just enough to drive me crazy with curiosity. The longer I listened, the more frustrated I got, and eventually I couldn't handle the not knowing one second longer. As quietly as I could, I slid out of bed, tiptoed to the door and opened it a crack. That was better.

"Oh, Gary — no! You're kidding!" my mother exclaimed in a whisper.

"No, I'm not. It's the truth," my dad replied. "I couldn't believe it either."

I didn't like the sound of that. I listened harder.

It was Mom again. "But why would he think — " And then she stopped so unexpectedly that I was sure I'd been discovered. But when she began speaking again, I knew I hadn't. "Good heavens — look at the time," she gasped. "It's nearly midnight! And you've got that early meeting tomorrow. Come on. We can talk about this in the morning."

The next thing I knew, there were footsteps coming down the hall toward me, so I tore back to bed and jumped under the covers.

But I didn't go to sleep. How could I?

All night long, I tossed and turned, worrying about the shred of conversation I'd overheard and wondering what it meant. Had something gone wrong? Had my dad discovered the truth? If the Mann had messed up the test somehow, he'd never ump again. Not only that, but my dad would think he was stupid — or dishonest! I couldn't decide which was worse.

All I knew for sure was that the test had been my idea, so either way it was my fault. And just thinking about it made me feel sick.

At 4:30 I peered at the clock by my bed. I was groggy, and my eyes burned from being open all night, but now I didn't want to fall asleep — not until I found out the truth about that test. Dad would be up in another hour and a half, and I would find out the answer then.

At least, I would have if I'd been awake.

CHAPTER 22

The alarm went off, and I sprang out of bed as if someone had fired a cannon beside my head. I'd had just enough sleep to know that I was exhausted, but not enough to help me think straight, and it was a good couple of minutes before the fog cleared. When it did, I sank down onto my bed in a discouraged heap and started to worry about the Mann and the test all over again. Only this time it was worse, because I'd had the whole night to stew about it, and by falling asleep, I'd blown my chance to get the truth from my dad. There was still Mom, though, I reminded myself as I struggled back to my feet and stumbled to the kitchen. But she was already on her way out the door to work. So I did the only other thing I could think of — I collapsed onto a chair and worried some more.

By the time I got to school I was a nervous wreck. Just the same, I didn't say a word to Kelly. It wouldn't have been fair. With Brian Billings coming to see him pitch, he had enough on his mind already. I didn't want to do anything to spoil his chances with that scout.

Besides, I might be worrying over nothing. For all I knew, my parents hadn't been talking about the Mann at all. They could have been discussing a completely different subject. That's what I told myself. The only problem was that I didn't believe me.

And I couldn't even ask the Mann what had happened. Not that I really wanted to. I mean, if something had gone wrong with the test, I didn't think he'd be very happy to see me. But I couldn't ask him anyway, because he wasn't there. According to the guy who was filling in for him, the Mann was at another school, fixing a broken boiler.

So I kept right on worrying. Oh, yeah — and sleeping. I kind of alternated between the two all day. A person can't really do any decent sleeping in a desk, but that didn't stop my eyes from flickering shut every half-hour or so. Considering I needed the rest, it should have been a good thing, except that right after my eyes closed, my muscles fell asleep too, and when that happened, my head would try to dive off my neck, my elbow would slide across the desk, and I would jolt awake agai — uusually to a bunch of snickering.

After school I went straight home. My mom

would be back from her job — she just works mornings — and I'd be able to ask her if she knew how the test had gone. Then I could crash on my bed until game time.

But Mom wasn't in the kitchen like I'd expected. In fact, she wasn't anywhere. The only sign that she'd been there at all was a note on the fridge.

Midge,
Dad is working until six, and I am at the dentist's. Your supper is in the microwave. Heat it for three minutes. We'll see you at the game.
Good luck. — Mom

Well, whatever had happened with the test, my parents still seemed to be speaking to me. Of course, that might only mean the Mann hadn't given me away, and so they didn't know what I'd done — yet.

I opened the door of the microwave. My spaghetti and wieners were inside, in a bowl covered with plastic wrap. I shut the door again. I'd never felt less like eating in my life. I was even having trouble worrying properly. I was simply too tired.

I shuffled to my bedroom. Hopefully I'd feel better after some sleep. The instant I saw my unmade bed, I knew just how Dorothy had felt in *The Wizard of Oz* when she'd run into that poppy field. It took all my willpower not to flop down and drift away. But I dragged myself to the alarm clock on my night table and set it for 5:45. The coach had told us to be at the park by 6:15 and, no matter how tired I was, I couldn't be late. Then I closed my eyes and let myself fall backwards onto the bed.

The train was bearing down on me, and I tried to jump off the track. But I couldn't. My runner was wedged beneath one of the ties, and no matter which way I wiggled it, I couldn't pry it free. I couldn't even pull my foot out of my shoe. Behind me the railway-crossing bell continued to clang its warning, and I frantically tugged at my foot some more.

The train was so close now I could see the engineer inside. He was blowing the horn and waving his arms. If I didn't get off that track, I was going to …

And then suddenly Kelly was beside me, reefing on the shoe too, trying to help me escape. Clang! Clang! The crossing bell nagged in the background, and the train loomed almost directly above us, blacking out the sky. I squeezed my eyes shut — I couldn't bear to look. But then Kelly gave one last mighty yank at my foot, and somehow it popped free — and the two of us rolled off the track.

"Midge, wake up!" Kelly shook me roughly, jiggling my eyes open.

Groggily, I looked around. The two of us were on the floor beside my bed — tangled in the sheets — and beside us on the night table my alarm clock was ringing up a storm.

"And turn off that darn clock!" He scowled, reaching over me to silence it. "Look at the time! What the heck are you doing sleeping? If we're late, Coach is going to kill us!"

I was still pretty dopey, but things were finally starting to make sense. As we disentangled ourselves from my bedding and each other, I asked, "How'd you get in here?"

"The front door," he said. "I rang the bell like twenty times. There was no answer. But I knew you had to be here — your bike is lying in the driveway — and besides, I could hear your alarm going crazy. So I tried the door." He shook his head. "You really ought to lock it, you know." Then he grinned. "You could get stolen."

I sank onto the bed and yawned.

"Hey, what are you doin'?" Kelly hauled me to my feet again. "We gotta get moving. You're not even dressed yet! Where's your uniform? Where's your glove? Where are your shoes?"

As Kelly ran around grabbing my stuff, the world slowly started coming into focus, and as it did, my drowsiness faded and adrenaline took over. By the time I was dressed, I was wide awake.

"All right." Kelly took one last look around the room and chucked my glove at me. "That's it. Let's go."

"Just one sec," I said, and took off to the kitchen.

"We haven't got a sec," Kelly complained, trailing after me.

I opened the microwave and took out the bowl. Then I peeled back the plastic wrap, grabbed a spoon and scooped up a wiener and a clump of spaghetti. *Ugh*. It just wasn't the same cold. But we were about to play the most important game of the season, and it was no time to mess with tradition.

So I choked down what was in my mouth and wiped my face on a dishtowel. "Okay," I said, throwing the towel onto the counter. "Let's go."

We were almost ten minutes late getting to the park, so naturally we were the last ones there.

"Where the heck have you two been?" Coach Bryant laid into us. "Don't you realize how important this game is?"

"Sorry, Coach," I apologized. "It's my fault. I fell asleep, and Kelly had to wake me up."

Coach Bryant looked like he needed to yell some more, but he held it in and just growled at us to get out on the field and warm up.

It felt good throwing the ball around, and anticipation of the game ahead completely chased away any tiredness I had left in my body. All I could think about was playing. I even forgot to worry about the Mann and that test.

The Demons had arrived too, and they were warming up on the other side of the field. It was still too early for fans, but one guy was already sitting in the bleachers. He had a really good tan and a clipboard that he kept writing on. I'd never seen him before, but I would've bet my starting spot on the team that it was Brian Billings.

CHAPTER 23

I hadn't thought about the Mann since I'd fallen dead asleep after school, but as the officials headed onto the field, all my fears came flooding back.

I tried to be logical. Even if the Mann wasn't one of the game's umpires, that didn't mean he'd blown the test. It just meant my dad hadn't changed the schedule. But in my heart I knew my father wanted the Mann umping as much as anyone. If the Mann had passed that test, my dad would have put him in.

Staring straight ahead from my seat in the dugout, all I could see were two pairs of black pant legs walking toward home plate. I told myself that one set belonged to the Mann. I wanted so much for that to be true that I almost believed it. Almost, but not quite.

I looked at the ump leading the way, and uneasiness began growing in my stomach. Clive Hollings was six-foot-four and skinny as a fence post. Even from the back, there was no confusing him with anybody else. My gaze shifted to the second umpire. He wasn't the Mann either, and the last of my hopes did a nosedive. I shut my eyes and leaned my head against the dugout's cold concrete wall.

Kelly elbowed me in the ribs. No doubt he wanted to know why the Mann wasn't umping, and I couldn't bring myself to explain. Not yet. Not when Kelly needed to stay focused. Not when he needed to play the game of his life. I fumbled around in my head for a way to put off his questions until later.

He jabbed me again.

"Kelly," I opened my eyes and began, "we knew from the start that this … " My words trailed off as I watched the Mann round the corner of the dugout and stride toward home plate with his face mask in his hand.

The people in the stands must've seen him at the same time I did, because one second they were sitting, waiting for the game to start, and the next second they were on their feet, clapping and whistling and whooping like crazy. And they wouldn't stop until the Mann finally lifted his hand in a self-conscious wave.

He was back!

Grinning his face off, Kelly elbowed me again,

and then he pummeled my shoulder. He was obviously happy — and I was glad about that — but if he got any happier, I was going to be one giant bruise.

Eventually things calmed down, and it was time to play ball. Since we were the home team, we took the field first. As I jogged into position, I glanced toward the bleachers where my dad always sits. He was right where he should be, smack dab behind home plate. And beside him was my mom, and beside her was Kelly's mom. It was a bit of a surprise to see my parents sitting together, but nothing compared to the shock I got as my eyes wandered to the next tier. Mrs. Butterman was sitting directly behind them! And in the row behind her was the scout from the Giants. The bunch of them were stacked one on top of the other, like a human totem pole.

Then the Mann shouted, "Play ball!" and the game got underway.

From the very start, it was tight. Kelly was pitching as good as I'd ever seen him. The Demons only got one hit off him, and that was from a bunt in the fourth inning. Luckily, they weren't able to turn it into a run.

But defensively, they were unreal. Coming off a win over the Lightning, the Demons were the only team in the playoffs who could afford a loss, and so they were taking chances they normally wouldn't. And it was paying off. Any time our team got a couple of runners on base, the Demons would make a monster play to keep us off the scoreboard. So by the end of the sixth inning, all we had was a one-run lead. It was still anybody's game.

In the seventh, the Demons came to bat with the top of their order. The first batter flied out, and Kelly struck out the next one. It looked like it was going to be a one, two, three inning. We would win without taking our last turn at the plate. And it should have turned out that way — except it didn't.

Kelly threw a fastball in on the hitter's hands, so he had no choice but to swing at it. He connected weakly, sending a routine grounder between second and third. I jogged over to first, snugged my foot against the bag and waited for Jerry to scoop up the ball and throw it to me. But just as it got to him, it took a bad hop and ricocheted off his mitt. Suddenly the tying run was on base.

After that, everything seemed to fall apart. The next batter was the Demons' best hitter, and though Kelly had won the match-up with him so far, this was no time to take any chances. One good crank of the bat, and we'd be on the losing end of the score. Better to walk him and increase our chances of a double play. So Kelly put him on.

With two out and runners at first and second, all Kelly needed to do was to put the ball in play. Us guys on the infield would do the rest.

The next batter came to the plate, and when he swung at the first two pitches, I got to thinking Kelly was just going to strike him out. The guy took a swing at the third pitch too. But this time he didn't miss. The ball came straight back like a bullet — right at Kelly's head.

Caught off-balance, all Kelly could do was stick up his hand — his pitching hand. The crowd gasped as the ball knocked him to the ground and then trickled toward first base. I tore off to get it, but it was too late to make a play. Now the bases were loaded. And our pitcher was down.

The Mann called time, and Coach Bryant shot out of the dugout. I walked the ball back to the mound to see how Kelly was.

He was on his feet again, massaging his hand and wiggling his fingers. There was a grimace on his face, but a look of determination too.

"I'm okay," he told Coach Bryant. "Nothing's broken. My hand's a little sore, but I can pitch. I just need a couple of minutes."

Coach didn't look too sure, but he didn't argue much. I didn't say anything. Kelly had pitched a great game. He didn't need to prove anything to anybody, and besides, I knew he would never jeopardize the team's chances. So if he said he could pitch, he must've thought he could.

But when he took the next batter to a full count and then lost him, walking in the tying run, I wasn't quite as sure. We were no closer to that final out, and now the game was tied.

The coach made another trip to the mound, but Kelly convinced him to leave him in for one more batter. If we didn't get the out, Kelly said he'd take himself out of the game.

The pressure was on. Everyone in the park could feel it. As the batter came to the plate, I moved a couple of steps further into the field than usual. With the bases loaded, there was no need to worry about holding the runner. The first two pitches were balls, and I wondered if Kelly had anything left, but when the next pitch whistled across the plate, I had my answer.

The batter swung late, but he still connected, sending the ball bouncing through no man's land between first and second. If it got past the infield, the Demons would score another run easily — probably two.

I leaped into the air, stretched out my glove and prayed.

Wham! Thwack! My body hit the dirt so hard, my head bounced, and I cracked my chin on the ground. My eyes rattled pretty good too. But there was no time to think about that. The ball was either in my mitt or halfway into the outfield, and since there was nothing I could do about it if it was there, I looked into my glove.

"Midge, throw it here!" Kelly yelled.

I didn't have time to get up. The best I could do was push up onto one knee and twist around. It wasn't much of a throw, but somehow Kelly caught it and beat the runner to the bag.

The Demons were out.

CHAPTER 24

But the game was far from over.

The coach hurried us off the field like a one-man cheerleading squad, clapping his hands, patting our backs and just generally rallying us on.

"That's it, boys! Way to dodge the bullet. Good heads-up play out there. Now, let's get those bats working. Pete, you're up," he said, checking his clipboard. Then he chucked a bag of ice at Kelly and said, "How's the hand?"

Kelly flexed it a couple of times. "It's okay."

Coach Bryant came in for a closer look.

"Like heck, it is." He frowned. "It's already starting to swell." He shook his head and squeezed Kelly's shoulder. "You pitched a great game, kid. Let's hope it was enough."

Then he squinted down the bench and hollered, "Peterson, you're pinch-hitting for Romani, so grab a bat. You're on deck." Then he turned to one of the other guys. "Latimer, start warming up. If this thing goes into extra innings, you're pitching."

Kelly's mouth dropped open.

"You're taking me out?"

"Sorry, pal," Coach Bryant said, "but I don't have a choice. We can't risk making that hand worse. We're going to need you for another game."

"But what about this game?" Kelly argued. "If we don't win this game, there won't be another one."

"Look at that hand!" Coach exclaimed. "There is no way you can pitch anymore. I like your spunk, but face it, Romani, you're done for the day. The other guys are going to have to pick up the slack."

"Okay, so I can't pitch," Kelly finally conceded, "but can't I at least take my turn at the plate? The Demons don't need to know I'm out of the game. Besides, I can still swing a bat. I know I can." But the coach seemed unconvinced. I guess Kelly sensed it too, because he added, "I just know I'm gonna get a hit, Coach. I can feel it. You gotta let me bat … *please*."

It didn't look like the coach was going to give in, but suddenly he blustered, "Oh, all right. You can bat." Then he shook a finger in Kelly's face. "But you're not pitching, Romani, and that's final."

Kelly grinned. "Don't worry, Coach — I won't need to."

Pete hit six or seven foul balls. The pitcher must

have been losing his stuff — or else he was getting tired. Either way, it was looking more and more like Pete was going to squeeze out a hit. But then he popped up right in front of home plate, and the catcher gloved the ball easily.

One out. We only had two chances left.

Kelly was up to bat, and I was on deck. I looked into the stands, wondering what Brian Billings was thinking of all this. Kelly had pitched a great game — the coach was right about that — so I didn't think Billings could be disappointed in that department. But I was curious to know what he thought of Kelly's injury. Would he be impressed that Kelly had played through it, or would he think that was a dumb move?

As I peered up at the crowd, the bat landed like a dead weight on my shoulder, and my eyes bugged out. Mrs. Butterman had moved up a row and was sitting right beside Brian Billings! Not only that, but she was talking up a storm and pointing to Kelly! And to make matters worse, Billings seemed to be all ears.

I wanted to rush over there and yell, *Don't believe a word she says! She hates Kelly.* But I knew I couldn't do that, so I forced myself to concentrate on the game. I pulled back my bat and waited for the pitch.

As the ball crossed home plate, I swung. Kelly didn't.

"Ball one," the Mann called out.

The catcher threw the ball back to the mound, and Kelly and I each took a couple more practice swings. The pitcher wound up and threw again. Again it missed the target.

"Ball two," the Mann announced.

Kelly was ahead of the count. That was okay too. A walk was as good as a hit. If Kelly got on base he would find some way to get home. And I'd do my best to help him, I told myself, swinging the bat with determination.

The next pitch was a fastball — high and inside. In fact, if Kelly hadn't hit the dirt it probably would have taken his head off.

The Mann put up his hands to stop play, and Kelly brushed himself off. He took his time getting back into the batter's box. The pitcher was trying to shake him up and, by stalling, Kelly was returning the favor.

It would be interesting to see what was going to happen with the next pitch. The count was 3 and 0, so Kelly should have been taking all the way. But I couldn't believe the Demons really wanted to walk him. The pitcher should be throwing a strike, and if he did …

Kelly and I both looked at the third-base coach for the signal.

The pitcher shook off the catcher's first two signs. Then he nodded, and went into his windup. The catcher held up his glove. The Mann got into his crouch. Kelly cocked his bat, and shifted his weight to his back foot. The pitcher threw the ball.

It was a good pitch — low and wide, but still in the strike zone — the kind of pitch that fools a batter. Maybe it's a strike; maybe it's a ball. You can't be sure. So if you're sitting with a 3 and 0 count, you probably leave it alone.

But if you're Cairo Kelly Romani and your team needs a run to stay in the playoffs — and you've got the green light — you swing with everything you've got.

Because the pitch was low, Kelly came up under it, and from the instant the bat made contact, the ball started to rise — just like a jet taking off. It seemed like it was still going up when it went over the head of the center fielder.

CHAPTER 25

The instant that ball left Kelly's bat, our entire team charged out of the dugout. So when Kelly crossed home plate, we were all over him. It was great! The public-address guy was hollering over the loud-speaker, we were mobbing Kelly, and the fans were cheering like we'd just won the World Series. The only thing missing was the fireworks. It was one of those moments you wish would last forever.

Eventually the excitement died down and the crowd started to thin out. That's when I noticed my parents and Ms. Romani standing beside our dugout. I grinned and waved, and my mom and Ms. Romani waved back. But my dad didn't even see me — probably because he was too busy staring at the backstop.

Actually, it wasn't the backstop he was staring at. It was Coach Bryant, the Mann and the scout from the Giants, who were standing in front of it.

The guys on my team had started to head back to the dugout, so I grabbed Kelly on the way by and pointed toward the three men. It just so happened that they chose that exact second to look our way too.

Coach Bryant motioned for Kelly to come over.

"I think that's your cue," I prompted Kelly when he didn't move.

"I guess," he mumbled, standing as still as ever.

"So get going. This is what you've been waiting for!" Then I gave him a shove. When I was sure he was finally on his way, I headed over to my parents.

"Oh, Midge!" Mom bubbled. "That was such an exciting game!" And for a second, I was afraid she was going to hug me — right on the ball field in front of everybody.

Ms. Romani smiled. "You played good, Meej."

"Nice diving stop you made out there, son," Dad added. "You saved the inning. Good work."

"Thanks." I lowered my eyes self-consciously.

Dad squinted at me. "So how's the chin? It looks like you're growing a green beard."

I groaned and spun away, almost crashing into Kelly, who had run up behind me and grabbed his mom's hand.

"What are you doing?" Ms. Romani pulled back in surprise.

"There's someone who wants to meet you, Ma."

Kelly's eyes were dancing. He pointed toward the backstop, and when Ms. Romani looked, the Mann waved.

"Go on, Connie," Mom encouraged her. "This is a mother's proud moment."

Ms. Romani still didn't look too sure, but she let Kelly lead her away.

Mom sighed the way she does when she's just finished reading one of her romance novels, and then she touched my dad's arm. "There's Barb Hart," she said, pointing across the field. "I'm just going to run over and talk to her about next month's community cookout. We're both on the refreshment committee. I won't be a minute." And then Mom was gone too.

There was just Dad and me left.

"Well, it certainly looks good," he said.

I turned to him in surprise. "What looks good?"

"The impression Kelly made on that scout," he replied.

"How do you know about the scout?" I demanded.

"The same way you do," he said. "Hal Mann and I had a little meeting the other night — remember? Or has that test slipped your mind already?"

An unexpected wave of guilt washed over me. I scrambled for something to say that wouldn't give me away. "So ... did he ace it?" I asked finally.

Dad scowled at me through his eyebrows. "Don't you know the answer to that already?"

"What do you mean?" I hedged, suddenly uneasy.

"Well, you're the one who's always saying how smart Hal is. Do you really think he would have had trouble with that test?"

I breathed a sigh of relief. For a second, I'd thought my dad was onto what I'd done. "No. Not really," I answered.

We were quiet for a bit, just long enough for me to let my guard down. Big mistake. Dad started talking again.

"Of course, he *would* have had trouble," he said casually, "if he'd written down the answers he'd memorized."

My knees turned to jelly. Dad *did* know about the test!

I knew he was waiting for me to say something, but I was so stunned, I couldn't speak.

Part of me just wanted to crawl away and hide. If the earth had split open right that second, I would have jumped into the nearest hole without thinking twice. But where's an earthquake when you really need one?

There was another part of me, though, that was totally calm. I had been discovered, and it was actually a relief not to have to pretend anymore.

"How did you know?" I asked quietly.

"Hal told me," Dad said. "The other night, just as I was about to give him the test. A different test, I might add, than the one you took from the filing cabinet. So if he'd written in the answers he'd memorized, he would have bombed it."

Suddenly I couldn't look at my dad. I felt so bad — not because I'd been caught, but because I could've gotten the Mann into trouble and because I knew I'd let my father down.

"Sorry," I mumbled. "I know it was wrong. It's just that I wanted to help the Mann."

Dad started talking again as if I hadn't said a word. "Hal also said that you tried to convince him to come clean. You told him that I would read the questions to him."

"But he didn't want to do that," I explained. "He didn't want you to know he couldn't read. He didn't want anyone to know."

"But more importantly, he didn't want you boys to get in trouble on his account," Dad pointed out.

"He did pass the test, though, didn't he?" I pushed. For some reason, I needed to be sure about that.

"Midge." Dad sounded impatient. "You and I both know there was never any doubt about that. Hal Mann is a great ump." He shook his head and sighed. "I suppose this whole thing is partly my fault. I should have nipped it in the bud when it first came up, but I didn't realize it was going to become such an issue. I guess I was hoping somebody else would take care of it. The thing is …"

He paused so long that I looked up. Something between amazement and bewilderment had taken control of his face. "I just never thought it would be you," he finished. "Not that what you did was right," he added quickly, and then his voice became less stern. "But your reasons certainly were. And that's a good starting place. The rest we can work on."

That's when Mom conveniently returned, and then Kelly and his mom came back too — and they were both all smiles.

"Well?" Dad rubbed his hands together and beamed at them. "How'd it go?"

"My son is going be a big shot baseball player!" Ms. Romani announced excitedly, making the rest of us laugh.

Kelly shook his head, but he was smiling. "*Maybe*, Ma," he told her. "*Maybe*. Nothing's for sure. Don't get carried away. Remember what Mr. Billings said. I gotta work hard. Nothing's for certain."

"But you go to college." His mom wagged her finger.

Kelly rolled his eyes and nodded. Then he explained, "Mr. Billings says that there are baseball camps I can attend during the summers — and there are assistance programs to help pay for them. He also says that I need to go to college and play ball there. He says that if I do well in school, there's a good chance I can get a baseball scholarship. After that ..." He shrugged. "Maybe I'll get drafted. In the meantime, Mr.

Billings is going to keep in touch with Coach Bryant and the Mann to see how I'm doing."

My mom gave Kelly a huge hug.

"Sorry, man," I apologized. But Kelly didn't seem to mind.

"This calls for a celebration!" Mom announced. "What do you say we all go for ice cream? My treat."

"Cool," I said, and everybody booed.

"What's all this commotion?" The Mann walked over to join us.

"Hey, Hal." My dad shook his hand. "It's good to have you back."

"It's good to be back," the Mann said, and then he turned to Kelly and me. "It looks like you two are glad to be back too. It was a pretty big night for you. Congratulations on your win. You both played a heck of a game."

Then he winked at Kelly and added, "Brian Billings was certainly impressed." And when Kelly grinned from ear to ear, the Mann shook his head. "Let's just hope he hasn't created a monster with an ego the size of a small continent. Midge, we're going to leave it up to you to keep this guy under control."

"Why do I always get the hard jobs?" I complained, and everybody laughed. When they'd stopped, I said, "Can I ask something?"

Kelly punched me in the arm. "I think you just did."

I ignored him and turned to the Mann. "I know that Brian Billings probably found out about Kelly through *Sport Beat* magazine. What I don't get is how *Sport Beat* found out about Kelly. But I'm betting you had something to do with it — right?"

The Mann laughed. "You're getting entirely too shrewd, Midge. If Kelly makes it to the majors, he might want to think about making you his agent." Then he nodded. "I've known Skylar Hogue for years. You might even say we used to be like brothers." He shrugged. "So I gave him a phone call."

"And the rest — as they say — is history," Dad grinned. Then he said, "We were just on our way for some ice cream to celebrate, Hal. Why don't you join us?"

The Mann shook his head. "Thanks for the invitation, but I'm afraid I can't. I have another engagement."

"Aw, c'mon," Kelly insisted. "Whatever it is, can't you do it some other time?"

"Nope," the Mann said firmly. "It's already waited far too long." Then he nodded across the diamond.

I couldn't believe my eyes. The Mann was turning us down for Mrs. Butterman!

"My teacher awaits," the Mann said sheepishly. "Tonight I get my first reading lesson." Then he waved and headed off across the field.

"You boys grab your things and hop on your bikes. We'll meet you at the ice cream place," Dad said. Then he and Mom and Ms. Romani started walking to the car.

As Kelly and I rounded up our stuff, my mind was going a million miles a minute. I didn't know what to think. I'd always hated Mrs. Butterman, but if she was going to teach the Mann to read, she couldn't be all bad — could she? Then I remembered her talking to Brian Billings during the game, and I changed my mind again.

I must've been scowling, because Kelly punched me in the arm. "She's not as awful as we thought," he said, reading my mind.

"Yeah, right," I retorted.

"No, really," he insisted. "The Mann says she's okay, and he's a pretty good judge of character." Then he grinned. "He likes *us,* doesn't he?"

"Ha, ha." I made a face. "You are too funny." And then I got serious again. "I don't know, Kel. I saw her talking to that scout during the game, and she was obviously telling him about you. And when has that ever been good?"

Kelly nodded. "I know. It's always seemed like she's been out to get us. But maybe she was just afraid that we were going to get her first."

We both kind of smirked.

"Anyway," he continued, "she told Mr. Billings that I have great leadership qualities."

My mouth dropped open. "Mrs. Butterman said that?"

Kelly nodded. "Yup."

I gave my head a shake. Life was getting entirely too complicated. You couldn't even tell the heroes from the villains anymore. Where were the good old days when all a guy had to do was play baseball and come up with a good excuse for not having his homework done? And if you did get caught doing something wrong, the worst thing that could happen was you got grounded or had to serve a detention. I'm not saying I was crazy about landing in hot water, but at least I understood the process.

Lately, though, I was getting sideswiped all over the place, and half the time it seemed like I was doing it to myself. Suddenly I had principles! I had a conscience! I was becoming responsible! Heck, the next thing I knew, I'd be getting a job!

That started me thinking.

"Hey, Kelly," I said, "About that agent thing … "

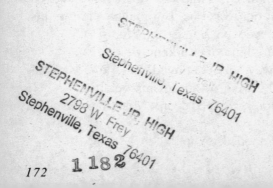

1182